SUGAR CREEK GANG
14
The TREASURE HUNT

Paul Hutchens

MOODY PUBLISHERS
CHICAGO

Original Title: *Sugar Creek Gang Digs for Treasure*

ISBN: 978-0-8024-7018-8
Printed by Bethany Press in Bloomington, MN – 1/2012

We hope you enjoy this book from Moody Publishers.
Our goal is to provide high-quality, thought-provoking
books and products that connect truth to your real needs
and challenges. For more information on other books
and products written and produced from a biblical per-
spective, go to www.moodypublishers.com or write to:

Moody Publishers
820 N. LaSalle Boulevard
Chicago, IL 60610

7 9 10 8

Printed in the United States of America

PREFACE

Hi—from a member of the Sugar Creek Gang!

It's just that I don't know which one I am. When I was good, I was Little Jim. When I did bad things—well, sometimes I was Bill Collins or even mischievous Poetry.

You see, I am the daughter of Paul Hutchens, and I spent many an hour listening to him read his manuscript as far as he had written it that particular day. I went along to the north woods of Minnesota, to Colorado, and to the various other places he would go to find something different for the Gang to do.

Now the years have passed—more than fifty, actually. My father is in heaven, but the Gang goes on. All thirty-six books are still in print and now are being updated for today's readers with input from my five children, who also span the decades from the '50s to the '70s.

The real Sugar Creek is in Indiana, and my father and his six brothers were the original Gang. But the idea of the books and their ministry were and are the Lord's. It is He who keeps the Gang going.

PAULINE HUTCHENS WILSON

1

I was sitting in a big white rowboat. It was docked at the end of the pier that ran far out into the water of the lake. From where I sat in the stern, I could see the two brown tents where the rest of the Sugar Creek Gang were supposed to be taking a short afternoon nap.

That was one of the rules about camp life none of us liked very well but which was good for us because then we always had more pep for the rest of the day and didn't get too tired before night.

I'd already had my afternoon nap and had sneaked out of the tent and to the dock, where I was right that minute. I was just sitting there and imagining things such as whether there would be anything very exciting to see if some of the gang could explore that big tree-covered island about a mile away across the water.

Whew! It certainly was hot out there close to the water with the sunlight pouring itself on me from above and also shining up at me from below. The lake was like a big blue mirror that caught sunlight and reflected it right up under my straw hat, making my hot freckled face even hotter. Because it was the style for people to get tanned all over, I didn't mind the heat as much as I might have.

It seemed to be getting hotter every minute, though. It was the kind of day we sometimes had back home at Sugar Creek just before some big thunderheads came sneaking up and surprised us with a fierce storm.

It was also a perfect day for a sunbath. *What on earth made people want to get brown all over for anyway?* I thought. Then I looked down at my freckled brownish arm and was disgusted with myself. Instead of getting a nice tan like Circus, the acrobatic member of our gang, I always got sunburned and freckled, and my upper arm looked like a piece of raw steak instead of a nice piece of brown fried chicken. Thinking that reminded me that I was hungry, and I wished it was supper time.

It certainly was a quiet camp, I thought, as I looked at the two tents where the rest of the gang was supposed to be sleeping. I just couldn't imagine anybody sleeping that long—anyway, not any boy—unless he was at home and it was morning and time to get up and do the chores.

Just that second I heard the sound of footsteps from up the shore. Looking up, I saw a smallish boy with brown curly hair coming toward me along the path that runs all along the shoreline. I knew right away it was Little Jim, my almost best friend and the greatest little guy that ever lived. I knew it was Little Jim not only because he carried his ash stick with him—which was about as long as a man's cane—but because of the shuffling way he walked. I noticed he was stopping every now and then to stoop over and look at some wild-flower. Then he'd write something down in a book he was carrying, which I knew was a wild-flower guidebook.

He certainly was an interesting little guy, I thought. I guess he hadn't seen me, because I could hear him talking to himself, which he had a habit of doing when he was alone. There was something kind of nice about it that made me like him even better than ever.

I think that little guy does more honest-to-goodness thinking than any of the rest of the gang—certainly more than Dragonfly, the pop-eyed member, who is spindle-legged and slim and whose nose turns south at the end; or Poet-ry, the barrel-shaped member, who reads all the books he can get his hands on and who knows 101 poems by heart and is always quot-ing one; and also even more than Big Jim, the leader of our gang, who is the oldest and who has maybe seventeen smallish strands of fuzz on his upper lip, which one day will be a mus-tache.

I ducked my head down below the dock so Little Jim couldn't see me and listened, still wondering, *What on earth!*

Little Jim stopped right beside the path that leads from the dock to the Indian kitchen, which was close by the two brown tents. He stooped down and said, "Hm! Wild strawberry." He leafed through the book he was carrying and wrote something down. Then he looked around him and, seeing a balm of Gilead tree

7

by the dock with some five-leaved ivy on it, went straight to the tree and with his magnifying glass began to study the ivy.

I didn't know that I was going to call out to him and interrupt his thoughts. That was something my mother had taught me not to do when a person is thinking hard, because nobody likes to have somebody interrupt his thoughts.

But I did. "Hi, Little Jim!" I said from the stern of the boat.

That little guy acted as cool as a cucumber. He just looked slowly around in different directions, including up and down. Then his blue eyes looked absentmindedly into mine, and for some reason I had the kindest, warmest feeling toward him.

His face wasn't tanned like the rest of the gang's. He was what people called "fair"; his small nose was straight, his little chin was pear-shaped, and his darkish eyebrows were straight across. His small ears were the way they sometimes were—lopped over a little because that was the way he nearly always wore his straw hat.

When he saw me sitting there in the boat, he grinned and said, "I'll bet I'll get an A in nature study in school next fall. I've found forty-one different kinds of wildflowers."

I wasn't interested in the study of plants at all right that minute. I was interested in having some kind of an adventure. I said to Little Jim, "I wonder if there are any different kinds of flowers over there on that island where Robinson Crusoe had his adventures."

Little Jim looked at me without seeing me, I thought. Then he grinned and said, "Robinson Crusoe never saw that island."

"Oh yes, he did! He's looking at it right this very minute and wishing he could explore it and find treasure or something," I answered, wishing I were Robinson Crusoe myself.

Just that second another voice piped up from behind some sumac on the other side of the balm of Gilead tree. "You can't be a Robinson Crusoe and land on a tropical island without having a shipwreck first, and who wants to have a wreck?"

I knew it was Poetry, even before he shuffled out from behind the sumac and I saw his round face and his heavy eyebrows that grew straight across the top of his nose, as if he had just one big long eyebrow instead of two like most people.

"You *are* a wreck," I called to him, joking. We always liked to have word fights that we didn't mean, after which we always liked each other even better.

"I'll leave you guys to fight it out," Little Jim said to us. "I've got to find me nine more kinds of wildflowers." With that, that little chipmunk of a guy scuffed on up the shore, swinging his stick around and stooping over to study some new kind of flower he spied every now and then.

And that's how Poetry and I got our heads together to plan a game of *Robinson Crusoe,* not knowing we were going to run into one of the strangest adventures we'd had in our whole lives.

"See here," Poetry said, grunting and sliding down off the side of the dock and into the boat where I was, "if we play *Robinson Crusoe*, we'll have to have one other person to go along with us."

"But there were only *two* of them," I said, "Robinson Crusoe himself and his man Friday, the boy who became his servant, and whom Crusoe saved from being eaten by the cannibals, and who, after he was saved, did nearly all Crusoe's work for him."

"All right," Poetry said, "I'll be Crusoe, and you be his man Friday."

"I will *not*," I said. "I'm already Crusoe. I thought of it first, and I'm already him."

Poetry and I frowned at each other.

Then his round face brightened, and he said, "All right, you be Crusoe, and I'll be one of the cannibals getting ready to eat your man Friday, and you come along and rescue him."

"But if you're going to be a cannibal, I'll have to *shoot* you, and then you'll be dead," I said.

That spoiled that plan for a minute, until Poetry's bright mind thought of something else, which was, "Didn't Robinson Crusoe have a pet goat on the island with him?"

"Sure," I said.

And Poetry said, "All right, after you shoot me, I'll be the goat."

Well, that settled that, but we couldn't decide right that minute the problem of which one of the gang should be the boy Robinson

Crusoe saved on a Friday and whom he named his man Friday.

It was Poetry who thought of a way to help us decide which other one of the gang to take along with us. It happened like this.

"Big Jim is out," I said, "because he's too big and would want to be the leader himself, and Robinson Crusoe has to be that."

"And Circus is out too," Poetry said, "on account of he's almost as big as Big Jim."

"Then there's only Little Jim, Dragonfly, and Little Tom Till left," I said.

Then Poetry said, "Maybe not a one of them will be willing to be your man Friday."

We didn't have time to talk about it any further. Right then Dragonfly came moseying out toward us from his tent, his spindly legs swinging awkwardly and his crooked nose and dragonflylike eyes making him look just like a ridiculous Friday afternoon, I thought.

"He's the man I want," I said. "We three have had lots of exciting adventures together, and he'll be perfect."

"But he can't keep quiet when there's a mystery. He always sneezes just when we don't want him to."

Dragonfly reached the pier and let the bottoms of his bare feet go *ker-plop, ker-plop, ker-plop* on the smooth boards, getting closer with every *ker-plop*.

When he spied Poetry and me in the boat, he stopped as if he had been shot at. He looked down at us and said in an accusing voice, "You guys going on a boat ride? I'm going along!"

I started to say, "Sure, we want you," thinking that, when we got over to the island, we could make a man Friday out of him as easy as pie.

But Poetry beat me to it by saying, "There's only one more of the gang going with us, and it might not be you."

Dragonfly plopped himself down on the edge of the dock, swung one foot out to the gunwale of the boat, caught it with his toes, and pulled it toward him. Then he slid himself in and sat down on the seat behind Poetry. "If anybody goes, I go, or I'll scream and tell the rest of the gang, and nobody'll get to go."

I looked at Poetry, and he looked at me, and our eyes said to each other, *Now what?*

"Are you willing to be eaten by a cannibal?" I asked, and he got a puzzled look in his eyes. "There're cannibals over there on that island— one, anyway—a great big barrel-shaped one that—"

Poetry's fist shot forward and socked me in my ribs, which didn't have any fat on them, and I grunted and stopped talking at the same time.

"We're going to play *Robinson Crusoe*," Poetry said, "and whoever goes will have to be willing to do everything I say—I mean everything *Bill* says."

"Please," Dragonfly said. "I'll do *anything*."

Well, that was a promise, but Poetry wasn't satisfied. He pretended he wanted Tom Till to go along, because he liked Tom a lot and thought he'd make a better man Friday than Dragonfly.

"We'll try you out," Poetry said and caught hold of the dock and climbed out of the boat.

The other two of us followed him.

"We'll have to initiate you," Poetry explained, as we all walked along together. "We can't take anybody on a treasure hunt who can't keep quiet when he's told to and who can't take orders without saying, 'Why?'"

"Why?" Dragonfly wanted to know.

But Poetry said with a very serious face, "It isn't funny," and we went on.

"What're you going to do?" Dragonfly asked, as we marched him along with us up the shoreline to the place where we were going to initiate him.

I didn't know myself where we were going to do it. But Poetry seemed to know exactly what to do and where to go and why, so I acted as though I knew too.

Poetry made me stop to pick up a big empty gallon can that had had prunes in it— the gang ate prunes for breakfast nearly every morning on our camping trip.

"What's that for?" Dragonfly asked.

And Poetry said, "That's to cook our dinner in."

"You mean—you mean—me?"

"You," Poetry said. "Or you can't be Bill's man Friday."

"But I get saved, don't I?" Dragonfly said with a worried voice.

"Sure, just as soon as I get shot," Poetry explained.

"And then you turn into a goat," I said, as he panted along beside us, "and right away you eat the prune can."

With that, Poetry smacked his lips as though he had just finished eating a delicious tin can. Then he leaned over and groaned as if it had given him a stomachache.

Right that second, I decided to test Dragonfly's obedience, so I said, "All right, Friday, take the can you're going to be cooked in and fill it half full of lake water!"

There was a quick scowl on Dragonfly's face, which said, *I don't want to do it.* He shrugged his scrawny shoulders, lifted his eyebrows and the palms of his hands at the same time and said, "I'm a poor heathen. I can't understand English. I don't want to fill any old prune can with water."

With that, *I* scowled and said to Poetry in a fierce voice, "That settles that! He can't take orders. Let's send him home!"

Boy, did Dragonfly ever come to life in a hurry! "All right, all right," he whined, "give me the can." He grabbed it out of my hand, made a dive toward the lake, dipped the can in, and came back with it filled clear to the top with nice clean water.

"Here, Crusoe," he puffed. "Your man Friday is your humble slave." He extended the can toward me.

"Carry it yourself!" I said.

And then, all of a sudden, Dragonfly set it down on the ground where some of it splashed over the top onto Poetry's shoes. Dragonfly got a stubborn look on his face and said, "I think the cannibal ought to carry it. I'm not even Friday yet—not till the cannibal gets killed."

Well, he was right, so Poetry looked at me and I at him, and he picked up the can, and we went on till we came in sight of the boathouse, which, if you've read *Screams in the Night,* you will already know about.

It was going to be fun initiating Dragonfly —just how much fun I didn't know. And I certainly didn't know what a mystery we were going to run into in less than fifteen minutes.

In only a little while we came to Santa's boathouse. Santa, as you know, was the owner of the property where we had pitched our tents. He also owned a lot of other lakeshore property up there in that part of the Paul Bunyan country. Everybody called him Santa because he was round like all the different Santa Clauses we'd seen, and he was always laughing.

Santa himself called to us with his big laughing voice when he saw us coming. "Well, well, if it isn't Bill Collins, Dragonfly, and Poetry." Santa, being a smart man, knew that if there's anything a boy likes to hear better than anything else it's somebody calling him by his name.

"Hi," we all answered him.

Poetry set down the prune can of water with a savage sigh as if it was too heavy for him to stand and hold.

Santa was standing beside his boathouse door, holding a hammer in one hand and a handsaw in the other.

"Where to with that can of water?" he asked us.

And Dragonfly said, "We're going to pour the water in a big hole up there on the hill and make a new lake."

Santa grinned at all of us with a mischievous twinkle in his blue eyes, knowing Dragonfly hadn't told any lie but was only doing what most boys do most all the time anyway—playing make-believe.

"May we look inside your boathouse for a minute?" Poetry asked.

And Santa said, "Certainly. Go right in."

We did and looked around a little.

Poetry acted very mysterious, as though he was thinking about something important. He frowned with his wide forehead and looked at different things such as the cot in the far end, the shavings and sawdust on the floor, and the carpenter's tools above the workbench—which were chisels, screwdrivers, saws, planes, and hammers and nails. Also, Poetry examined the different kinds of boards made out of beautifully stained wood.

"You boys like to hold this saw and hammer a minute?" Santa asked us. He handed a hammer to me and a saw handle to Dragonfly, which we took, not knowing why.

"That's the hammer and that's the saw the kidnapper used the night he was building the grave house in the Indian cemetery," Santa said.

I felt and must have looked puzzled till he explained, saying, "The police found them the night you boys caught him."

"But—but how did they get *here*?" I asked.

Poetry answered me by saying, "Don't you remember, Bill Collins, that we found this boathouse door wide open that night—with the latch hanging? The kidnapper stole 'em."

I looked at the hammer in my hand and remembered. I tried to realize that the hammer I had in my hand right that minute was the same one that, one night last week, had been in the wicked hand of a very fierce man who had used it in an Indian cemetery to help him build a grave house. Also, the saw in Poetry's hand was the one the man had used to saw pieces of lumber into the right lengths.

"And *here*," Santa said, lifting a piece of canvas from something in the corner, "is the little nearly finished grave house. The lumber was stolen from here also. The police brought it out this morning. They've taken fingerprints from the saw and hammer."

"Why on earth did he want to build an Indian grave house?" I asked, looking at the pretty little house. It looked like the chicken coop we had at home at Sugar Creek, only almost twice as long.

Dragonfly spoke up then and said, "He maybe was going to bury the little Ostberg girl there."

But Poetry shook his head. "I think he was going to bury the ransom money there, where nobody in the world would guess to look."

Well, we had to get going with our game of *Robinson Crusoe,* which we did, all of us feeling fine to think that last week we had had a chance to catch a kidnapper, even though the ransom money was still missing.

2

I had a weird feeling as we left the boathouse and went up the narrow, hardly-ever-used road to the top of the hill. Then we followed that road through a forest of jack pine and along the edge of a little clearing. I was remembering what exciting things had happened here the very first night we'd come up North on our camping trip.

I think Poetry was remembering too, because he said in a ghostlike voice to make the atmosphere of Dragonfly's initiation seem even more mysterious to him, "Right here at this sandy place in the road is where the car was stuck in the sand. And right over there behind those bushes is where Bill and I were crouching half scared to death, watching him."

"Yeah," I said, "and he had the little Ostberg girl he'd kidnapped right in the backseat of the car all the time, and we didn't know it."

"How'd he get his car *un*stuck?" Dragonfly wanted to know, even though the whole Sugar Creek Gang had probably been told a dozen times by Poetry and me.

So I said, "Well, his wheels were spinning and spinning in the sand, and he couldn't make his car go forward. But it would rock forth and back, so he got out and let air out of his back tires till they were almost half flat. That made them wider and increased traction. And then, when he climbed back into his car and stepped on the gas, why he pulled out of the sand and went *lickety-sizzle* right on up this road."

"You going to initiate me *here?*" Dragonfly asked.

I started to say, "Yes," but Poetry said, "No, a little farther up, where we found the little girl herself."

We walked along in the terribly sultry afternoon weather. Pretty soon we turned off the road and came into a little clearing that was surrounded by tall pine trees. I was remembering how right here Poetry and I had heard the little girl gasping out half-smothered cries. And with our flashlights shining right on her, we'd found her lying wrapped up in an Indian blanket.

"She was lying right here," Poetry said, "right here where we're going to initiate you." Poetry's ordinarily ducklike voice changed to a growling bear's voice. He sounded very fierce.

There really wasn't anything to worry about out here, though. We knew the police had caught the kidnapper, and he was in jail somewhere, and the pretty little golden-haired Ostberg girl was safe and sound with her parents again back in St. Paul.

"But they never did find the ransom money," Poetry said, which was the truth. "And nobody knows where it is. But whoever finds it gets a thousand dollar reward—a whole thousand dollars!"

"You think maybe it's buried somewhere?" Dragonfly asked with a serious face.

"Sure," Poetry said. "We're going to play *Robinson Crusoe* and *Treasure Island* both at once. First we save our man Friday from the cannibals, and then we quit playing *Robinson Crusoe* and change to *Treasure Island*."

Well, it was good imagination and lots of fun, and I was already imagining myself to be Robinson Crusoe living all by myself on an island. In fact, I sometimes have more fun when I imagine myself to be somebody else than when I am just plain red-haired, fiery-tempered, freckled-faced Bill Collins.

It was fun the way Poetry and I initiated Dragonfly into our secret game—anyway, fun for Poetry and me. This is the way we did it.

I hid myself out of sight behind some low fir trees with a stick in my hand for a gun. Poetry stood Dragonfly up against a tree and tied him with a piece of string he carried in his pocket.

"Now, don't you dare break that string!" Poetry told him. "You're going to be cooked and eaten in a few minutes! You can pretend to try to get loose, but don't you dare do it!"

I stood there hiding behind my fir trees, getting ready to shoot with my imaginary gun just in time to save Dragonfly from being cooked.

Dragonfly did look funny standing there tied to the tree and with a grin on his face, watching Poetry stack up a little pile of sticks for our imaginary fire. We wouldn't start a real fire. Nobody with any sense starts a fire in a forest, because then there might be a terrible forest fire. Thousands of beautiful trees could be burned, and lots of wild animals, and maybe homes and cottages, and even people themselves.

When the stack of sticks was ready, Poetry set the big prune can on top. Then he turned to Dragonfly and started to untie him.

"Groan!" Poetry said to him. "Act like you're scared to death! Yell! *Do* something!"

Dragonfly didn't make a very scared native boy. "There's nothing to be afraid of," he said.

And there wasn't, I thought.

But all of a sudden there was. As soon as Poetry had Dragonfly cut loose, he dragged him toward the imaginary fire. Dragonfly was making it hard for him by struggling and hanging back and making his body limp so that Poetry had to almost carry him. And just as I peered through the branches of my hideout and pointed my stick at Poetry and was getting ready to yell, *"Bang! Bang!"* before rushing in to rescue Dragonfly, there was a crashing noise in the underbrush behind me.

I heard footsteps running and then a loud explosion that sounded like a gun going off, which almost scared the living daylights out of me—and also out of the poor boy and the cannibal that was getting ready to eat him.

When I heard that shot behind me, I jumped almost out of my skin, I was so startled and frightened. Poetry and poor little pop-eyed Dragonfly acted as if they were scared even worse than I was.

When you're all of a sudden scared like that, you don't know what to say or think. Things sort of swim in your head, and your heart beats fiercely. Maybe we wouldn't have been quite so frightened if we hadn't had so many important things happen to us already on this camping trip, such as finding the little kidnapped girl in this very spot the very first night we'd been up here—and then the next night catching the kidnapper himself in a spooky Indian cemetery.

I was prepared to expect almost anything when I heard that explosion and the crashing in the underbrush. And then I could hardly believe my astonished eyes when I saw right beside Dragonfly and Poetry a little puff of bluish-gray smoke, and I knew that somebody had thrown a firecracker right in the middle of our excitement.

"It's a firecracker!" Dragonfly yelled.

And then I had an entirely new kind of scare. I saw a little yellow flame where the explosion had been. And then I saw some of the dry pine needles leap into flames, and the flames start to spread fast.

I knew it must have been one of the gang who'd maybe had some firecrackers left over from the Fourth of July at Sugar Creek.

Quicker than I can write it for you, I dashed into the center of things, grabbed up our prune can full of water, and in seconds had the fire out.

Then, seconds later, I heard a scuffling behind me and a grunting and puffing. Looking around quick—the empty prune can was still in my hands—I was just in time to see Circus scramble out of Poetry's pudgy hands and go shinnying up a tree, where he perched himself on a limb and looked down at us, grinning like a monkey.

I was mad at him for breaking up our game of make-believe and for shooting off a firecracker in the forest, where it might start a terrible fire. So I yelled up at him and said, "You crazy goof! Don't you know it's terribly dry around here and you might burn up the whole Chippewa Forest?"

"I was trying to help you kill a cannibal," Circus said. But he had a hurt expression in his voice and on his face as he added, "Please don't tell Barry I was such a dumbbell." Barry was our camp director.

I forgave Circus right away when I saw he was really trying to join in our fun and just hadn't used his head, not thinking of the danger of forest fires at all.

"You shouldn't even be carrying matches to light a firecracker with," Poetry said up at him.

"Every camper ought to have a waterproof matchbook with matches in it," Circus said. "I read it in a book that told what to take along on a camping trip. Besides," he said down to us, "we can't play *Robinson Crusoe* without having to eat, and how are we going to eat without a fire?"

I knew then that he'd guessed what game we were playing and had decided to go along.

"We don't need you," I said. "We need only my man Friday and a cannibal that gets killed—"

"And turns into a goat," Poetry cut in to say.

"Only *one* goat would be terribly lonesome," Circus said. "I think I ought to go along. I'd be willing to be another goat."

Well, we had to get Dragonfly's initiation finished, so I took charge of things and said, "All right, Poetry, you're dead! Lie down over there by that tree. And you, Dragonfly, get down on your knees in front of me and put your head clear down to the ground."

"Why?" Dragonfly asked.

And I said, "Keep still. My man Friday doesn't ask, 'Why?'"

Dragonfly looked a little worried. But he did as I said and bowed his head low in front of me with his face almost touching the ground.

"Now," I said, "take hold of my right foot and set it on the top of your neck—*no!*" I yelled down at him. "Don't ask, 'Why?' Just do it!"

Dragonfly did.

"And now, my left foot," I ordered.

"That's what the boy did in *Robinson Crusoe,* so Crusoe would know he thanked him for saving his life from the terrible cannibals and that he would be his slave forever," I said to Dragonfly. "Do you solemnly promise to do everything I say from now on and forevermore?"

Dragonfly started to say, "I do," but got only as far as "I—" when he started to make a funny little sniffling noise. His right hand let loose of my foot, and he grabbed his nose and went into a tailspin kind of sneeze. He ducked his neck out of the way of my foot and rolled over and said, "I'm allergic to your foot."

The dead cannibal on the ground thought that was funny, and he snickered, but I saw a little blue flower down there with pretty yellowish stamens in its center, and I knew why Dragonfly had sneezed.

My man Friday, rolling over, tumbled *kersmack* into the cannibal. The two of them forgot they were in a game and started a friendly scuffle, just as Circus slid down the tree and joined in with them. All of a sudden Dragonfly's initiation was over.

He was my man Friday, and from now on he had to do everything I said.

Up to now it was only a game we'd been playing. But a minute later Circus rolled over and over, clear out of reach of the rest of us, and scrambled up into a sitting position. He said to us excitedly, "Hey, gang, look! I've found something—here at the foot of the tree. *It's a letter of some kind!*"

I stared at the old envelope in Circus's hands, remembering that right here was exactly where we'd found the kidnapped girl. I remembered that the police hadn't been able to find the ransom money and that the captured kidnapper hadn't told them where it was.

In fact, he had absolutely refused to tell them. We'd read that in the newspapers.

Boy oh boy, when I saw that envelope in Circus's hands, I imagined all kinds of things, such as its being a ransom note, or maybe it had a map in it that would tell us where we could find the money and everything! Boy oh boy oh boy oh boy!

3

When you have a mysterious sealed envelope in your hand, which you've just found under some pine needles at the base of a tree out in the middle of a forest, and when you're playing a game about finding buried treasure, all of a sudden you sort of wake up. You realize that your game has come to life and that you're in for an honest-to-goodness mystery that will be a thousand times more interesting and exciting than the imaginary game you've been playing.

We decided to keep our assigned names, even though we had an argument about it first. I was still Robinson Crusoe, and Dragonfly was my man Friday. Circus and Poetry wanted us to call them the cannibals, but Dragonfly wouldn't.

"I don't want to have to worry about being eaten up every minute," he said. "You've got to turn into goats right away anyhow. Besides, one cannibal's already been shot and is supposed to be dead."

"You'd make a good goat yourself," Circus said to me. "A *Billy* goat, because your name's Bill."

But it wasn't any time to argue, when there was a mysterious envelope right in the middle of our huddle at the base of the tree where Circus had found it.

Poetry said, "All right. I'll be the goat if you let me open the envelope."

"And I'll be the other goat," Circus said, "if you'll let me read it."

"Let *me* read it," Dragonfly said to me. "Goats can't read."

"You can't read either," I said. "You're a native boy who doesn't know anything about civilization, and you don't know how to read."

So it was I who got to open the soiled brown envelope, which I did with excited fingers, and then we all let out four disappointed groans. Would you believe it? There wasn't a single thing written on the folded white paper inside—not one single thing. It was only a blank piece of typewriter paper.

Well, that was that. We all sank down on the ground in different directions. I felt as though the bottom had dropped out of our new mystery world. I looked at Friday, and he looked at me. And the roly-poly goat started chewing his cud, while my acrobatic goat rolled over on his back, pulled his knees up to his chin, and groaned. Then he rolled over onto my man Friday, which started a scuffle, making my man Friday angry.

All of a sudden Dragonfly remembered something about the story of Robinson Crusoe. He grunted and said, while he twisted and tried to get out from under the goat, "Listen, you—when Robinson Crusoe and his man Friday got hungry, they killed and ate one of the goats. And if you don't behave yourself like a good goat, we'll—"

But Circus was as mischievous as anything and said, while he rolled himself back toward Dragonfly again, "Isn't your name Friday?"

Dragonfly grunted and said, "Sure."

And Circus answered, "All right. I'm sleepy, and there's nothing better than taking a nap on Friday," which he pretended to do. He shut his eyes and started snoring as loud as he could, which sounded like a goat with asthma.

That reminded Poetry of something funny he'd read somewhere. It was about two fleas who were supposed to have lived on the island with Robinson Crusoe and his man Friday. Both of these fleas had been chewing away on Crusoe and were getting tired of him and wanted a change. So pretty soon one of them called to the other and said, "So long, kid, I'll be seeing you on Friday."

I barely giggled at Poetry's story, because my mind was working hard on the new mystery. I was thinking about the blank piece of paper, and why it was blank, and why the envelope was sealed, and who had dropped it here, and when, and why.

So I stood up and walked the way Robinson Crusoe might have walked, in a little circle around the tree, looking up at the limb where Circus had been perched and then at the ground. I looked at Poetry, my roly-poly goat, who right then unscrambled himself from the rest of the inhabitants of our imaginary island and followed me around, sniffling at my hand like a hungry goat that wanted to eat the letter I held.

Abruptly Poetry stopped and said to me, "*Sh!* Look, here's a sign of some kind."

I looked but didn't see anything except a small branch about four or five feet long that was broken off and had been left with the top hanging.

My man Friday and the acrobatic goat were still scuffling under the tree and didn't seem interested in what we were doing.

"What kind of a sign?" I asked, knowing that Poetry was the one of our gang who was more interested in woodcraft than most of the rest of us and was always looking for signs and trails and things.

"See here," he said to me, "this is a little birch branch, and somebody's broken it part way off and left it hanging."

"What of it?" I said, remembering that back home at Sugar Creek I'd done that myself to a chokecherry branch or a willow, and it hadn't meant a thing.

"But look which way the top points!" Poetry said mysteriously. "That means it's a signal on a trail. It means for us to go in the direction the top of the broken branch points, and after a while we'll find another broken branch, and whichever way it points we're to go that way!"

Say, did my disappointed mind ever come to quick life! I still doubted it might mean anything, but right away we called the other goat and my man Friday and let them in on our secret. Then we all started off, pretending to be scouts, going straight in the direction the broken branch pointed, all of us looking for another broken branch farther on.

We'd walked about twenty yards through the dense growth before we found another broken branch hanging, *but we did find one.* This time it was a broken oak branch, and it was bent in the opposite direction we'd come from, which meant the trail went straight on. Then we did get excited, because we *knew* we were on somebody's trail.

My man Friday was awfully dumb for one who was supposed to be used to outdoor life, though. He wanted to finish breaking off the top of the oak branch and cut off the bottom and make a stick out of it to carry and to take home with us back to Sugar Creek when we finished our vacation.

"For a souvenir," he whined complainingly, when we wouldn't let him and made him fold up his knife and put it back into his pocket.

"That's the signpost on our trail!" Poetry explained. "We have to leave it there so we can follow the trail back to where we started from, or we might get lost."

I thought that was good sense and said so.

We scurried along, getting more and more interested and excited as we found one broken branch after another. Sometimes they were pointing straight ahead and sometimes at an angle. Once we found one broken clear off and lying flat on the ground, at a right angle from the way we'd been traveling, so we turned in the direction it pointed and kept going.

Another time when Poetry was studying very carefully the direction a new broken branch was pointing, he gasped and said, "Gang! Look at this!"

We scrambled to him like a flock of little fluffy chickens making a dive toward a mother hen when she clucks for them to hurry to her and eat a bug or a fat worm.

"See here," Poetry said. "Here's where our trail goes off in two directions—one to the right and the other to the left."

He was right. Only a few feet apart were two broken branches, one an oak and the other a chokecherry. The chokecherry was pointing to the right and the oak to the left.

"Which way do we go for the buried treasure?" Poetry asked me, and I didn't know what to answer.

Then Poetry let out a gasp and said, "This one pointing to the right looks like it's fresher than the other. We certainly are getting the breaks."

We all studied the two broken branches, and I saw that Poetry was right. The one pointing to the right did look a lot fresher than the one pointing to the left. *Why, it might even have been broken off today!* I thought. And for some reason, not being able to tell for sure just how long it had been since somebody had been right here making the trail, I got a very peculiar and half-scared feeling all up and down my spine.

"I wish Big Jim was here," my man Friday said.

I wished the same thing, but instead of saying it, I said bravely, "Who wants Big J—" and stopped as if I had been shot at and hit. I'd heard a sound from somewhere, a sound that was like a high-pitched, trembling, woman's voice calling for help. It also sounded a little like a screech owl's voice, wailing along Sugar Creek at night.

"It's just a loon," Circus said and was crazy enough to let out a long, loud wail that trembled and sounded more like a loon than a loon's wail does.

I looked at my man Friday and at my roly-poly goat to see what they thought it was. Right away, before I could read their thoughts, there was another trembling, high-pitched voice that answered Circus. The second I heard it, I thought, *That didn't sound like a loon but like an actual person calling and crying and terribly scared.*

You can't hear a thing like that out in the middle of the Chippewa Forest, where there are different kinds of wild animals, and not feel like I felt, which was almost half scared to death for a minute. I knew there weren't any bears or lions in the forest—only deer and polecats and coons and possums and maybe mink, but . . .

"It's *not* a loon," I whispered huskily and

felt my knees get weak. I wanted to plop down on the ground and rest. I also wanted to run.

Then the call came again not more than a hundred feet ahead of us. And as quick as I *had* been scared, I *wasn't* again, for this time it did sound exactly like a loon.

Right away we all felt better and said so to each other.

The newest broken branch was pointing in the direction the sound came from, so we decided there was probably a lake right close by, which is where loons nearly always are—out on some lake somewhere, swimming along like ducks and diving and screaming bloody murder to their mates.

We plodded along, being very careful to look at the broken branches so we'd remember what they looked like when we got ready to come back.

My roly-poly goat and I were walking together ahead of my man Friday and my acrobatic goat. We dodged our way around fallen tree trunks and old stumps and around wild rosebushes and wild raspberry patches and chokecherries. And still there wasn't any lake anywhere.

I certainly had a strange feeling, though, as we dodged along, talking about our mystery and wondering where we were going and how soon we would get there.

"It's funny how Circus found that envelope way back there with only a blank piece of white paper in it," I said. "Do you s'pose the kidnapper dropped it when he left the little Ostberg girl there?"

"I suppose—why, sure, he did," Poetry said.

"How come the police didn't find it there, then, when they searched the place last week for clues? If it'd been there then, wouldn't they have found it?" I asked those two questions as fast as I could, because it seemed that envelope in my pocket was hot and would burn a hole in my shirt any minute.

Poetry's forehead frowned. He was as stuck as I was over the mystery.

In fact, all our minds seemed as blank as the blank letter. Not a one of us could think of anything that would make it make sense, so we went on, following our trail of broken twigs. What we were doing was fun, and we didn't feel *very* scared because we knew the kidnapper was in jail.

In fact, I think we were all thrilled with the excitement. For some reason, we were sure we might find something terribly interesting at the end of the trail, if we ever came to it. We didn't know that we'd not only find something very interesting but would bump into an experience even more exciting and thrilling than the ones we'd already had on that camping trip—one that was just as dangerous.

We came to a hill. I looked ahead and spied a wide expanse of blue water down below us. On the hillside between us and the lake was a log cabin. It had a big log door and a chimney running up the side next to us. We all saw it at once, I guess, because we all dropped down behind some underbrush and most of us said, "*Sh!*" at the same time.

We lay there for what seemed a terribly long time before any of us did anything except listen to ourselves breathe. I was also listening to my heart beat. But not one of us was as scared as we would have been if we hadn't known that the kidnapper was all nicely locked up in jail and nobody needed to be afraid of *him*.

I guess I'd not had such a wonderful feeling for a long time as I did right that minute. I realized that we'd followed the trail like real scouts and we'd actually run into the kidnapper's hideout. And we might find the ransom money. Boy oh boy oh boy oh boy!

Why, all we'd have to do would be to go up to that old-fashioned-looking house, push open the door, and look around until we found it, I thought.

It was certainly a weathered old house, and it looked as if nobody had lived in it for years and years. The windows had old green blinds hanging at crooked angles. Some of the stones had fallen off the top of the chimney, and the doorstep was broken down and looked rotten. I could tell from where I stood that there hadn't been anybody going through *that* door for a while because there was a spider web spun from the doorpost next to the old white knob to one of the up-and-down logs in the middle of the door.

"Let's go in and investigate," Poetry said.

"Let's n–not," my man Friday said.

And I scowled at him and said fiercely, "Slave, we're going in!"

4

Even though there was a spiderweb across the door, which probably meant that nobody had gone in or out of the door for a long time, still that didn't mean there might not be anybody inside. There might be another door on the side next to the lake.

Poetry and I made my man Friday and the acrobatic goat stay where they were while we circled the cabin, looking for any other door and any signs of somebody living there. The only other door we found was one that led from the cabin out onto a screened front porch. But the porch was closed in and had no door going outside, because there was a big ravine just below the front of the house and between it and the lake.

So we knew that if anybody wanted to go in and out of the house, he would have to use the one and only door or else go through a window.

We circled back to Dragonfly and Circus. Then we all lay down on some tall grass behind a row of shrubbery that somebody years ago had set out when maybe a family had lived there. It had probably been someone's summer home, I thought. Somebody who lived in St. Paul or Minneapolis or somewhere had built the cabin up here.

I noticed that there was a cement walk running all around the back side of the cabin, which was set up against the clifflike hill. Also, a long stone stairway began about twenty feet from the spiderweb-covered door and ran around the edge of the ravine, making a sort of semicircle down to the lake. On the shore I saw an old dock, which the waves of the lake in stormy weather, or else the ice in the winter, had broken down, and nobody had fixed it.

We waited in our hiding place for maybe ten minutes, listening and watching, before we decided nobody was inside. We decided to look in the windows and later go inside ourselves.

We didn't think about that being trespassing, because there was an old abandoned house back at Sugar Creek that our gang went into anytime we wanted to. Nobody thought anything about it, because the house belonged to a long-whiskered old man whom everybody knows as Old Man Paddler. Anything that belonged to him seemed to belong to us too, since he was a very special friend of anybody who was lucky enough to be a boy.

Anyway, soon we were peeking in through the windows, trying to see what we could see, but it was pretty dark inside. We knew that if we wanted to see more we had to find some way to get in.

I decided to see if my man Friday was my man Friday or not, so I said, "OK, Friday, go up and knock at that door."

Well, Dragonfly got the most scared look

on his face. As you maybe know, Dragonfly's mother believed in ghosts and in good luck from finding a four-leaf clover or a horseshoe. Dragonfly believed it too. Most boys believe and do what their parents believe and do.

Dragonfly not only had a scared look on his face but also a stubborn one. He said, "I *won't*."

He refused to budge an inch, so in a very fierce voice I commanded Poetry and Circus, "OK, cannibals, eat him up!"

"They're not cannibals!" Dragonfly whined. "They're goats, and goats only eat tin cans and shirts and things like that!"

"What's the difference?" the roly-poly goat said and started headfirst for Dragonfly.

But we couldn't afford to waste time that way, so Poetry, being maybe the bravest one of us, went up to the door, while we held our breath. I *knew* that there wasn't anybody inside but wondered if there was—and if there was, who was it, and was he dangerous, and what would happen if there was a fierce man in there.

First Poetry brushed away the spiderweb. Then he knocked on the door.

Nobody answered, so he knocked again and called, "Hello! Anybody home?"

He waited, and so did we, but there wasn't any answer. So he turned the knob, twisting it this way and that, and the door didn't open. He turned around to us and said, "It's locked."

Well, I had it in the back of my mind that the ransom money might be in that cabin and that we ought to go in and look—as I told you, not thinking that it was trespassing on somebody's property to go in without permission.

We found a window on the side of the cabin right next to the hill, which on that side of the house was kind of like a cliff. That window, when we tried it, was unlocked.

"You go in and unlock the door from the inside and let us in," I said to my acrobatic goat, and he said, "It's private property."

Well, that second I felt a drop of rain on my face, and that's what saved the day and made it seem all right for us to go inside. We all must have been so interested in following the trail of broken branches and in our game of *Robinson Crusoe* that we hadn't noticed the lowering sky and the big thunderheads that had been creeping up. Only a few seconds after that first drop of rain splashed onto my freckled face, there was a rumble of thunder, then another, and it started to rain.

We could have ducked under some trees for protection, but it was that kind of rain that seems as if the sky has burst open and water just drives down in blinding sheets.

"It's raining pitchforks!" Circus yelled above the roar of the wind in the trees. He quick shoved up the window and scrambled in.

All of us scrambled in after him and slammed down the window behind us.

The rain was coming down so hard that it made a terrible roaring on the shingled roof, reminding me of storms back at Sugar Creek when I was in the haymow of our barn. If there was anything I liked to hear better than almost anything else, it was rain on a shingled roof. Sometimes when I was in the upstairs of our house, I would open the attic door on purpose just to hear the friendly noise the rain made.

It was darkish inside the old cabin because the walls were stained with a dark stain of some kind, maybe to protect the wood, the way some north woods cabins are. It was also dark because the sky outside was almost black with terribly heavy rain clouds. I noticed that the window we'd climbed through was the kitchen window and that there was a table with a few dirty dishes over next to the wall. Also there was a white enameled sink and an old-fashioned pitcher pump like the one we have outdoors at our house at Sugar Creek.

The main room, where the fireplace was, was in the center of the cabin and was so dark you could hardly see anything clearly at first. But I did see two big colored pictures on the back wall.

We didn't even bother to look around inside the cabin for a while—anyway, I didn't. I hurried out onto the porch at the front, just to get a look at the storm. Storms are one of the most interesting sights in the world. They make a boy feel strange inside, as if maybe he isn't very important. They also make him feel that he needs the One who made the world in the first place to sort of look after him, which is the way I felt right that minute.

I noticed that there was a sheer drop of

maybe fifteen feet right straight down into the ravine, and I remembered that if anybody wanted to get out of the cabin by a *door*, he'd have to use the only one there was, which was the one that had been locked when Poetry had tried the knob.

I also noticed there were two or three whiskey bottles on the front porch. One with the stopper still in it was half full, standing on a two-by-four ledge running across the front.

I could see better out there, although the terribly dark clouds and also the big pine trees all around with their branches shading the cabin made it kind of dark even on the porch. Two big colored pictures were on the back wall of the porch. The pictures were advertising whiskey and showed important-looking people drinking or getting ready to.

Circus had come out, and I looked at him out of the corner of my eye, remembering how his dad used to be an alcoholic before he had trusted the Lord Jesus to save him. Circus was looking fiercely at those pictures, and I noticed he had his fists doubled up, as though he wished he could sock somebody or something terribly hard. I was glad right that minute that Little Tom Till wasn't there, because his daddy was still an alcoholic and a mean man.

I left Circus looking fiercely at those whiskey pictures, and I turned toward the lake. It was a pretty sight. The waves were being whipped into big whitecaps and were blowing and making a noise, which, mixed up with the noise on

44

our roof, was very pretty to my ears. Away out on the farther side of the lake there was a patch of sunlight, and the water there was all different shades of green and yellow.

Suddenly there was a terrific roar as a blinding flash of lightning lit up the whole porch, and then it *did* rain. The wind blew harder and whipped the canvas curtains on the porch, and the pine trees between us and the lake acted as if they were going to bend and break. Six white birch trees, which grew in a cluster down beside the stone stairway, swayed and twisted. *They* acted as though they were going wild and might be broken off and blown away any minute.

"Hey! *Look!*" Circus said. "There are little moving mountains out there on the lake!"

I looked, and that was what it did look like. The wind had changed its direction and was blowing parallel with the shore, instead of toward it, and other high waves were trying to go at right angles to the ones that were coming toward the shore. It was a terribly pretty sight.

All of a sudden, while standing there and feeling a little bit scared because of the noise and the wind and the rain, I got to thinking about my folks back home. And then I was lonesome as well as scared.

Also I was thinking that my parents had taught me that all the wonderful and terrible things in nature had been made and were being taken care of by the same God who had made growing boys—and that He loved everybody and was kind and had loved people so much that He had sent His only Son into this very pretty world to die for all of us and to save us from our sins. My parents believed that and had taught it to me.

And nearly every time I thought about God, it was with a kind of friendly feeling in my heart, knowing that He loved not only all the millions of people in the world but also *me*—all by myself—red-haired, fiery-tempered, freckled-faced Bill Collins, who was always getting into trouble, or a fight, or doing something impulsive and needing somebody to help me to get out of trouble.

Without knowing I was thinking out loud, I did what I sometimes do when I'm all by myself and have that very friendly feeling toward God. I said, "Thank You, dear Savior, for dying for me. You're a wonderful God to make such a pretty storm."

I didn't know Dragonfly was standing there beside me, until he spoke up all of a sudden and said, "You oughtn't to swear like that. It's wrong to swear."

All the gang knew it was, and none of us did it. Little Jim especially couldn't stand to even *hear* swearing without getting a hurt heart.

"I didn't swear," I said to Dragonfly. "I was just talking to God."

"You *what*?"

"I was just telling Him it was an awful pretty storm."

"You mean—you mean you aren't afraid to talk to Him?"

Imagine his saying that! But then, he hadn't been a Christian very long and didn't seem to understand that praying and talking to God are the same thing, and that everybody ought to do it, and if your sins have been washed away, then there isn't anything to be afraid of.

I was aroused from what I'd been thinking by my acrobatic goat calling to us from back inside the cabin, saying, "Hey, gang! Aren't we going to explore this old shell and see if we can find the ransom money?"

That brought me back in a hurry from where my mind had been for a few minutes.

I took another quick look at the little moving mountains on the lake, and pretty soon we were all inside where Circus had been looking around to see what he could find.

It was too dark to see anything very clearly in the main room, and we didn't have any flashlight. I looked on the high mantel above the fireplace to see if there was any kerosene lamp, but there wasn't. There wasn't any furniture in the main room except a table, three small chairs, and one big old-fashioned Morris chair like one my dad always sat in at home in our living room. It had a fierce-looking tiger head with a wide-open mouth on the end of each wooden arm, which gave me an eerie feeling when Circus lit one of his matches.

"There's a candle out on the kitchen table," Dragonfly said and brought it in to where we were.

There was only a stub of candle left. It wouldn't burn long. But Circus lit it while Poetry held it, and then we followed Poetry all around wherever he went.

It certainly was the darkest cabin on the inside that I'd ever seen. The brown walls were almost black, and the stone arch at the top of the fireplace was black from smoke. The noise of the storm and the darkish cabin made it seem we were having a strange adventure in the middle of the night.

There was dust on things, and it looked as if nobody had lived here for an awfully long time, maybe years and years. There were just three rooms: the kitchen with the sink and pitcher pump, the main room with the fireplace, and a small bedroom, which had a curtain hanging between it and the main room. In the bedroom was a roll-away bed all folded up and leaning against a wall.

Even though the broken twig trail had led us to this place, still we couldn't find a thing that looked like the ransom money might have been hidden here. So, since the rain was still pouring down, we decided to call a meeting and talk things over.

We pulled the three hardback chairs up to the table in the center of the main room. I turned the big Morris chair sideways and sat on one of the wooden arms. Poetry set the flickering candle in a saucer in the center of the table, and I, the leader, called the meeting to order, just the way Big Jim does when the gang is all present. It felt good to be the leader, even though I knew I wasn't and Poetry would have made a better one.

We talked all at once and also one at a time part of the time, and not one of us had any good ideas as to what to do—except, when the storm was over, to follow our trail of broken branches back to where the girl had been found and from there to camp.

I looked at Poetry's broad face, and at Dragonfly's large eyes and crooked nose, and at Circus's monkey-looking face, and we all looked at each other.

All of a sudden Poetry's forehead puckered, and he lifted his head and sniffed two or three times. He said, "You guys smell anything funny, like—kinda like a dead chicken or something?"

I sniffed a couple of times—we all did. And as plain as the nose on my face I did smell something—something dead. I'd smelled that smell many a time back along Sugar Creek when there was a dead rabbit or something else and the buzzards were circling around in the sky or had swooped down and were eating it.

Dragonfly's dragonflylike eyes looked startled, and I knew that if I could have seen mine in a mirror, they'd have looked just as startled.

"It smells like a dead possum carcass that didn't get buried," Circus said. He especially knew what *they* smell like, because his pop catches many possums and sells the fur. Sometimes when his father catches a possum, he skins it before going on and leaves the carcass in the woods or in a field.

It was probably a dead animal of some kind, we decided, and went right on with our meeting, talking over everything from the beginning up to where we were right that minute—the kidnapping, the found girl, the police who had come that night and made a plaster of paris cast of the kidnapper's tire tracks, and the kidnapper himself, whom we'd caught in the Indian cemetery.

"Yes," Poetry said, "but what about the envelope with the blank piece of typewriter paper in it?"

There wasn't any sense in talking about *that* again. We'd already decided it had maybe been left there by the kidnapper, who had planned to write a note on it and had gotten scared and left it, expecting to come back later. Anyway, anything we'd said about it didn't make sense, so why bring it up again?

"That's out," I said. "I'm keeping it for a souvenir." I had it in my shirt pocket and for fun pulled it out and opened it and turned it over and over in my hands to show them that it was as white as a Sugar Creek pasture after a heavy snowfall.

But as I spread it out, Poetry let out an excited gasp and exclaimed, "Look! There *is* something written on it!"

I could hardly believe my eyes, but there it was as plain as day, something that looked like writing—scratches and crooked lines and long straight lines and down at the bottom a drawing of some kind.

5

You can imagine how we felt when we suddenly saw that almost illegible drawing on paper that, when we'd found it, had been without even one pencil mark on it. Now as plain as day there *was* something on it. But we saw it wasn't drawn on with pencil or ink or crayon but looked sort of like what is called a "watermark," which you can see on different kinds of expensive writing paper.

All of us leaned closer, and I held it as close to the smoking and flickering candle as I could so that we could see it better.

Then Poetry gasped again and said, "Now it's getting plainer. Look!"

And right in front of our eyes as I held the paper near the candle, the different lines began to be clearer, although they still looked like watermarks.

Dragonfly turned as white as a sheet. His eyes almost bulged out of his head. "There's a–a–a *ghost* in here!" He whispered the words in such a ghostlike voice that it seemed there *might* be one.

For a minute I was as weak as a cat, and my hands holding the paper were so trembly that I nearly dropped it. In fact, as quick as a flash, Poetry grabbed my hand and pulled the paper away from the candle, or it might have touched it and caught fire.

Whatever was going on didn't make sense. My brain sort of whirled, and I sniffed again. I thought of something dead, and then of the writing that was on the paper and hadn't been before, and about Dragonfly's idea that there was a ghost in the old cabin. I wished I were outside in the rain running *lickety-sizzle* for camp and getting there right away.

But it was Poetry who solved the problem for us by saying, "It's invisible ink, I'll bet you. Being in Bill's pocket next to his body made it warm, and now the heat from the candle is bringing out even more what was written on it."

It took only moments to see that Poetry was right. As we all looked at the strange drawing, I was sure we'd found a map of some kind and that if we could understand it, and follow it, we would find the kidnapper's ransom money.

Poetry took out his pencil, and, because the lines weren't any too plain in some places, he started to trace them. Then he gasped and whistled and said, "It's a map!"

When he got through tracing it, we saw that it was a map of the territory right around where we were. Different places were named, such as the Indian cemetery, the fire warden's cabin, the boathouse, two summer resorts, the different roads running from one to another, and the names of the different lakes, on one of which we had our camp.

We all crowded around the table, looking

over Poetry's shoulders, all feeling mysterious, I think, and also a little bit scared. But not much, because I was remembering that the kidnapper was locked up in jail and couldn't get out.

"What's that X there in the middle for?" my man Friday wanted to know.

And Poetry said, "That's where we initiated you," and there was a mischievous sound in his ducklike voice.

"What?" I said. I was beginning to get a letdown feeling.

Dragonfly burst out with a savage sigh and said, "I might have known there wasn't any mystery. You made that map yourself."

By now I was thinking the same sad thing, and said so.

But Poetry shushed us and said, "Don't be funny. That's where Bill and I found the little Ostberg girl."

"Yeah," Dragonfly said, "but that's also where Robinson Crusoe stepped on my neck!"

"Oh, all right," Poetry said. "That's a dirty place on your neck which needs washing."

But Dragonfly didn't think that was funny, which maybe it wasn't very.

Just a little distance above the X, we noticed there was a big V, a drawing of a broken twig, and a line pointing toward the cabin where we were right that minute. Also a line ran from the top of the other arm of the V off in another direction until it came to a drawing that looked like a small mound. Lying across that was a straight short line that made me think of a walking stick.

It didn't make sense until I noticed that Poetry's pencil had missed tracing part of it, so I said, "Here, give me your pencil. There's a little square on the end of this straight line."

I made the square. Then I saw there was a small circle at the opposite end of the straight line. So I traced that, and the whole map was done.

It was Circus who guessed the meaning of the square and the circle at opposite ends of the straight line. He said. "It's a shovel or a spade! That circle is the top of the handle, and the square is the blade."

We knew he was right. And that meant, as plain as the nose on Dragonfly's face, that if we left this house and went back to where our trail had branched off and followed the broken twigs in that *other* direction, we'd come to the place where the money was buried.

Boy oh boy oh boy! I felt so good I wanted to scream. It was just like being in a dream, which you know isn't a dream—and you're glad it isn't. Only in dreams you always wake up, which maybe I'd do in just another excited minute.

"Is this a dream or not?" I asked my roly-poly goat.

And he said, "I don't know, but I know how I can find out for you," and I said, "How?" and he said, "I'll pinch you to see if there is any pain, and if there is, it *isn't*, and if there *isn't*, it is." He was trying to be funny and not being, because right that second he pinched me, and it hurt as it always does when he pinches me, only worse.

"Ouch!" I said, and right away I pinched *him,* so he could find out for himself that the map wasn't any dream and neither was my hard pinch on his arm.

The rain was still pounding on the roof, sounding like a fast train roaring past the depot at Sugar Creek. We all sat looking at each other with weird expressions on our faces and mixed-up thoughts in our minds. And then the candle burned out.

I was still smelling the dead something-or-other. The odor seemed to come from the kitchen, which was on the side of the cottage next to the steep hillside. Right above its one window I noticed there was a stubby pine tree growing out of the hill, its branches extending over the roof.

Because the rain wasn't blowing against the window, I opened it and looked out. Water was streaming down the hill like a little river, pouring onto the cement walk and rippling around the outside of the cabin. I thought how smart the owners of the cabin had been to put that cement walk there, so the water that gushed down the hillside could run away and not pour into the house.

It was while I was at the window that I noticed an old rusty wire stretched across from the stubby pine tree toward the cabin. I yelled to the rest of the gang to come and look, which they did.

"It's a telephone wire," Dragonfly said.

Poetry, squeezing in between Dragonfly and me and looking up at the wire, said, "I'll bet it's a radio aerial!" His voice got excited right away, and he turned back into the kitchen. "There might be a radio around here somewhere!" With that he started looking for one.

We helped him, going from the kitchen to the darkish main room, where the fireplace was, and through the door curtains into the bedroom, which had the roll-away bed in it, all folded up against the wall. Then we hunted through the screened porch and looked under some old canvas on the porch floor, but there wasn't any radio anywhere.

"There's got to be one," Circus said. "That's an aerial, I'm sure."

Poetry spoke up and said, "If it is, let's look for the place where it comes into the cabin."

We did, and we found it. It was through the top of a window in the bedroom. But that didn't clear up our problem even a tiny bit, because there was only a piece of twisted wire hanging down from the curtain pole, and it wasn't fastened to anything.

Well, that was that. Besides, what'd we want to know whether there was a radio for? "Who cares?" I said, feeling I was the leader and wishing Poetry wouldn't insist on following out all *his* ideas.

"Goof!" he said to me, which was what he

was always calling me, but I shushed him and said, "Keep, still, Goat! Who's the head of this treasure hunt?"

He puckered his forehead at me and half yelled above the roar of the rain on the roof, "If there's a radio, it means somebody's been living here just lately."

"And if there isn't, then what?"

It was Dragonfly who saw the edge of a newspaper sticking out from between the folded-up roll-away bed in the corner. He quick pulled it out and opened it.

We looked at the date, and it was just a week old! In fact, it was dated the day before we'd caught the kidnapper, so we were pretty sure he'd been here at that same time.

Well, the rain on the roof was getting less noisy, and we knew that pretty soon we'd have to be starting back to camp. We wouldn't dare try to follow the trail of broken branches to the place where we thought the money was buried, because we had orders to be back at camp an hour before supper time to help with the camp chores. That night we were going to have a very special campfire service with Eagle Eye, an honest-to-goodness Chippewa Indian, telling us a bloodcurdling story of some kind—a real live Indian story.

"Let's get going," I said to the rest of us, "just the minute it stops raining."

"Do we go out the door or the window?" my man Friday asked.

I took a look at the only door and saw that it was *nailed* shut, tighter than anything.

I grunted and groaned and pulled at the knob, then gave up and said, "Looks like we'll use the window."

It was still raining pretty hard, and I had the feeling I wanted to go out and take a last look at the lake. I'd been thinking also that if this cabin was fixed up a little and the underbrush between it and the lake and the battered old dock was cleared away, and if the walls were painted a light color, it might make a nice cabin for somebody to rent and spend a summer vacation in, the way a lot of people in America do.

On the wall of the porch I noticed a small mirror. It was dusty and needed to be wiped off before I could see myself. I stopped just a second to see what I looked like, as I sometimes do at home, especially just before I make a dash to our dinner table. Sometimes I get stopped before I can sit down. Then I have to go back and finish washing my face and combing my hair before I get to take even one bite of Mom's great fried chicken.

I certainly didn't look much like the pictures I'd seen of Robinson Crusoe. Instead of looking like a shipwrecked person with homemade clothes, I looked just like an ordinary wreck without any ship. My red hair was mussed up, my freckled face was dirty, and my two large front teeth still looked too big for my face, which would have to grow a lot more before it was big enough to fit my teeth. I was glad my teeth were already as big as they would ever get—which is why lots of boys and girls look funny when they're just my size, Mom says. Our teeth grow in as large as they'll ever be, and our faces just sort of take their time.

"You're an ugly mutt," I said to myself and then turned and looked out over the lake again. Anyway, I was growing a *little* bit, and I had awfully good health and felt wonderful most of the time.

While I was looking out at the pretty lake, some of the same feeling I'd had before came bubbling up inside of me. For a minute I wished Little Jim had been with us. In fact, I wished he were standing right beside me with the stick in his hand that he almost always carries wherever he goes.

I was feeling good inside because the gang was still letting me be Robinson Crusoe and was taking most of my orders. *Sometime,* I said to myself, *I'd like to be a leader of a whole lot of people, who would do whatever I wanted them to.* I might be a general in an army, or maybe a governor. But I wanted to be a doctor, too, and help people to get well. Also I wanted to help save people from their troubles and from being too poor, like Circus's folks. And I wished I could take all the whiskey there was in the world and dump it into a lake, except that I wouldn't want the perch and northern pike or walleyes or the pretty bluegills or bass or sunfish to have to drink any of it. Maybe I wouldn't care if some of the bullheads did.

While I was standing there, thinking about that pretty lake and knowing that Little Jim, the best Christian in the gang, would say something about the Bible if he was there, I remembered part of a Bible story that happened out on a stormy, rolling lake just like this one. Then I remembered that in the story of Robinson Crusoe there had been a Bible and that he had taught his man Friday a lot of things out of it and Friday had became a Christian himself.

My dad used to read *Robinson Crusoe* to Mom and me many a night in the winter. Dad read good stories to us instead of letting me listen to whatever there was on the radio that wouldn't be good for a boy to hear, and my folks having to make me turn it off. Dad always picked a story to read that was interesting to a red-haired boy and would be what Mom called "good mental furniture"—whatever that was or is.

All of the gang nearly always carried New Testaments in our pockets. So, remembering that Robinson Crusoe had had a Bible, I took out my New Testament and stood with my back to the rest of the cabin, still looking at the lake. I felt terribly good inside with that little brown leather Testament in my hands. I was glad that the One who is the main character in it was a Friend of mine and that He liked boys.

"It was great of You to help us find the little Ostberg girl," I said to Him, "and also to catch the kidnapper. And it's an awful pretty lake and sky and—"

Right then I was interrupted by *music* coming from back in the cabin somewhere. I heard some people's voices singing a song I knew and that we sometimes sang in church back at Sugar Creek. It was:

Rescue the perishing, care for the dying,
Jesus is merciful, Jesus will save.

I guessed quick that one of my goats or else my man Friday had actually found a radio in the cabin and had turned it on. I dashed back inside and through the curtains into the bedroom where I'd left them, where what to my wondering eyes should appear but the rollaway bed opened out. There, sitting on the side of it, were my two goats and my man Friday with a little portable radio. It was on my rolypoly goat's lap and was playing like a house afire that very pretty church hymn:

Down in the human heart, crushed by the
    tempter,
Feelings lie buried that grace can restore.

As I got there, the music stopped, and a voice broke in and said, "Ladies and gentlemen, we interrupt this program to make a very important announcement. There is a new angle regarding the ransom money still missing in the Ostberg kidnapping case. Little

Marie's father, a religious man, has just announced that the amount represented a sum he had been saving for the past several years to build a memorial hospital in the heart of Palm Tree Island. In St. Paul, the suspect, caught last week near Bemidji by a group of boys on vacation, still denies knowing anything about the ransom money. He claims he never received it. Police are now working on the supposition that there may have been another party to the crime. Residents of northern Minnesota are warned to be on the lookout for a man bearing the following description: He is believed to be of German descent, about thirty-seven years of age, six feet two inches tall, weighs one hundred eighty pounds, is stoop-shouldered, has a dark complexion and red hair, is partly bald, has bulgy steel-blue eyes, bushy eyebrows . . ."

The description went on, but I didn't need any more. My heart was already bursting with the most awful feeling I'd had in a long time, because the person they were describing was exactly like old hook-nosed John Till!

John Till was the mean, liquor-drinking father of one of the Sugar Creek Gang, little red-haired Tom Till himself—one of my very best friends, whom all of us liked and felt terribly sorry for.

We knew that Tom had the kind of father who had been in jail lots of times and who spent his money on whiskey and gambling. We knew that his mother had to be sad most of the time. In fact, about the only happiness his mom had was in her boy Tom, who was a really great little guy and went to Sunday school with us. She also got a little happiness out of a radio that my folks had bought for her, and she listened to Christian programs, which cheered her up a lot.

Even while I listened to the radio that was on my roly-poly goat's lap, I was thinking about Little Tom's mom and wondering if she had her radio turned on back at Sugar Creek and would hear this announcement, and if it would be like somebody jabbing a knife into her heart and twisting it.

But we didn't have time to think or talk or anything else. Suddenly I heard a noise coming from the direction of the kitchen window that we had climbed in. I took a quick peek through the door curtains, and I saw the face of a fierce-looking man. It took me only one second's glance to see the bushy eyebrows that met in the center just above the top of his hooked nose. And even though he had on a battered felt hat that was dripping wet and his clothes were sopping, I recognized him as Little Tom's father.

I remembered the first time I had seen John Till. He'd been hired by my dad to shock oats, and he had tried to get Circus's dad to take a drink of whiskey. It had been a terribly hot day, and Circus and I had been helping shock oats too. Circus's pop hadn't been a Christian very long, and because I didn't want him to do what is called "backslide," I had made a terribly fast run across the field to try to stop him from taking the drink. I'd run *ker-wham,* with both fists flying, straight into John Till's stomach. A little later I'd landed on my back under the elderberry bushes after a fierce *wham* from one of John Till's hard fists.

After that, the gang had had a lot of other trouble with John Till, but we'd seen Little Tom saved, and Tom had been praying for his dad every day since. Up to now it looked like praying hadn't done any good. His father still was a bad man and caused his family a lot heartache.

Talk about mystery and excitement! I knew Tom's dad hated us boys. Also he was pretty mean to Tom for going to church with us, and on top of *that* he was mad at my folks for taking Tom's mom to church. Whenever he came into the house and she had a Christian program on the radio, he would either make her turn it off or he would turn it off himself.

I'll have to admit that I was afraid of old hook-nosed John Till. And right then I didn't feel much like being the leader of the gang, which for some reason all of a sudden seemed to be made up of only four very small boys. The only thing I felt like leading was a very fast footrace out through the woods and toward camp.

"Quick!" I whispered. "There's somebody looking through the kitchen window. What'll we do?" Before anybody could answer, I saw the man's hand shove up the window. One of his wet long legs, which had a big wet shoe on the end of it, swung over the window ledge, and he started squirming his long-legged self in after it.

6

Well, what can you do when there isn't a thing you can think of doing? When you are looking through an opening in a curtain and see a mean man coming into your cabin? And when you know there isn't any door you can dash through to get away?

Poetry already had the radio shut off, and all of us were as still as scared mice, listening. Also, all of us were trying to peep through the opening in the curtain.

I noticed that John Till had a new-looking fishing rod, which he stood against the wall by a window. Then he turned his back, reached out of the window, and bent over to pick up something that he had left out there. A moment later I saw what it was—a stringer of fish, looking like five or six big walleyed pike and an extra large northern pike, which he probably caught out in the lake.

He lifted the stringer, and I heard the fish go *ker-flippety-flop-flop* into the sink. Then the iron pitcher pump squeaked as if he was pumping water on the fish, maybe to wash the dirt and slime off of them.

The curtain we were peeping through looked like the material one of my mom's chenille bedspreads is made out of. It was sort of fuzzy on one side. Even before I heard Dragonfly do what he did just then, I was afraid he would do it. He had his face up close to the curtain, not far from mine, and all of a sudden he got a puzzled expression on his face, his eyes started to squint, his mouth to open, and he made a quick grab for his crooked nose with one of his hands.

But it was too late. Out came a loud sneeze, which he tried to smother and didn't. It sounded the way his sneezes nearly always sound—like a Fourth of July firecracker that didn't explode but just went *ssss-sh-sh* instead.

John Till jumped as if he'd been shot at and hit. He whirled around and looked through the main room and at the curtain behind which we were hiding. If it had still been raining hard, he wouldn't have heard us, maybe, but Dragonfly's sneeze seemed to have been timed with a lull in the rain. In spite of the fact that it was a smothered hissing noise, the sneeze was loud enough to be heard.

I expected most anything terribly exciting and dangerous to happen.

First, John Till took a wild look around as though he wanted to make a dash for a door or a window and disappear. He must have thought better of it, though, because then he fumbled at his belt, and in a second I saw in his right hand a fierce-looking knife, just like the kind Barry carried. Its wicked-looking blade was about five inches long and looked as if it could either slice a fish into steaks or do the same to a boy.

Not a one of us had any weapons except our pocket knives. And also not a one of us was going to be foolish enough to start a fight. If only we could make a dash for the door and get out—*if the door wasn't nailed shut,* I thought. Then we could run like scared deer and get away.

But there wasn't a chance in the world—not against a fierce man with a fierce-looking hunting knife in his hand.

Then big John Till's voice boomed into our room and said, "All right, whoever you are. Come out with your arms up!"

"What'll we do?" Dragonfly's trembling whisper asked me, but I already had my arms up, and in a second he had his spindly arms pointed in different directions toward the ceiling.

"Get 'em up!" I whispered to all of us. If we got a chance, I thought, we could make a dive for the open kitchen window and head for camp terribly fast.

But Poetry's forehead was puckered with a very stubborn pucker, and before I knew what he was going to do, he yelled, "Come on out on the porch and get us!"

Of course, we weren't on the front porch, and it didn't make sense at all until a little later.

As you know, Poetry's voice was changing. Part of the time it was a bass voice, and the other part of the time it was a soprano, because he was old enough to be what my dad called an "adolescent." Part of what Poetry said was in a man's voice and sounded pretty fierce, but right in the middle of the sentence his voice changed, and it was like a scared woman's voice, the kind that would have made Dragonfly think it was a ghost's voice if he had heard it in the middle of a dark night in an old abandoned house.

To make matters worse, Dragonfly sneezed again, and we knew we were found out for sure.

Maybe John Till really thought we *were* out on that front porch. All of a sudden he left the sink, where he'd been pumping water on his fish. With his big knife in his hand, he charged out of the kitchen and through the main room, dodging the table and the Morris chair, and made straight for the porch.

And that was our signal to make a run for the kitchen and the open window. Poetry let the baby-sized radio plump down on the rollaway bed. Even as I led the mad dash to the window, I noticed that the radio's side panel had dropped open. And that was what turned it on.

Most of us got to the window at the same time. My acrobatic goat grabbed the kitchen table and shoved it into the doorway between the kitchen and the main room to block John Till's way if he tried to come back quick and stop us. Poetry was out first, then Dragonfly, then Circus, and Robinson Crusoe last of all. In the seconds the others took to get out, I got a glimpse of the big stringer of fish John Till had caught and which was right that second covered with water in the sink. The northern pike was especially very pretty. Before I left the North this summer, I wanted to catch a big fish, have it mounted by a taxidermist, and then put it on the wall of my room back at Sugar Creek.

I didn't understand why John Till—as soon as he found out we *weren't* out on that porch but had tricked him—didn't come dashing madly back and jump over the table in the doorway and grab the last ones of us to get through the window. But he didn't, and I was too scared to stop to find out why.

We raced around the corner of that cabin, made four dives in the direction we knew the broken-twig trail went, and sped through the still-sprinkling rain, through the wet shrubbery, and under the trees that were dripping water like a leaky roof, and headed for camp.

Was I ever glad we had our trail of broken branches to go by. When we got to the first one, Dragonfly, whose feet were getting wet, as were all of ours, stopped and made a grab for his nose. I knew he was allergic to something— maybe to wet feet. When he'd finished his sneeze, he said, sniffing at something he couldn't see, but which he knew was there, "I still smell something—*d–dead!*—something in that direction over there!"

I sniffed in that direction, and there was that same dead smell that we'd smelled in the cabin. But this time it was mixed up with the friendly odor of a woods after a rain.

My roly-poly goat smelled in the same direction, and so did my acrobatic goat, and we all smelled the same very unpleasant odor of something dead.

"I wonder who it is," Poetry said, and Dragonfly looked as if he was thinking about a ghost again.

And then I heard music coming from somewhere—in fact, from the direction of the cabin we'd been in, and I knew it was the radio, which had plopped open when my roly-poly goat had left it in a hurry. Though I couldn't hear the words, I recognized the tune, and it was "Since Jesus Came into My Heart."

We hurried on, following our trail, happy that we had managed to get out of trouble so easily. But we wondered aloud to each other if old hook-nosed John Till had had anything to do with the kidnapping, if maybe he knew where the ransom money was, and why he hadn't come rushing back into the kitchen to catch us.

"I think I know why," Circus said. "He's just like my dad was before he was saved. He couldn't stand to see a bottle of whiskey without taking a drink. And I'll bet when he saw that half-empty bottle out on the porch, he just grabbed it up and started gulping it down."

Then Circus, being a little bashful about talking about things like that, as some boys sometimes are, looked up at the tree limb extending out over where he was going to walk. He leaped up and caught hold of it with his hands. He chinned himself two or three times, while Dragonfly, who was beside him under the leaves of that branch, let out a yell and said, "Hey, watch out! Quit making it rain on me!"

That is exactly what Circus had done. The leaves of that branch got most of the water shaken off, and a lot of it fell all over Dragonfly.

We hurried on, talking and asking questions and trying to figure out what on earth the deadish smell was. Also we were wishing we had all the Gang with us, and a shovel, and time to follow the other trail of broken branches and actually find the ransom money right now.

In a little while we came to the place where we'd first found the envelope with the invisible-ink map in it. There we stopped for a minute and looked all around to be sure we would remember the place when we came back.

And about twenty minutes later, we came puffing into camp in sunshiny weather. The sky had cleared after the storm, but we were as wet as drowned rats.

The minute the others saw us come sloshing up to our tents, Big Jim called out, "Where on earth have you been?"

Well, we'd agreed to keep our secret a secret for a while. At least we'd not tell Barry right away. Sooner or later we would tell the rest of the gang—except Tom Till. We might decide to tell Tom too, but we wouldn't if Big Jim said not to, because it might spoil Tom's vacation, and then he wouldn't have any fun the rest of our camping trip.

Dragonfly answered Big Jim's questions in a mischievous voice by saying, "Bill's been walking on my neck, and Poetry and Circus have been making soup out of me, and I am a native boy," which wouldn't make sense to anyone who didn't know about Crusoe, his man Friday, and the cannibals.

As soon as we could, we changed to dry clothes, and Big Jim took command of us by saying, "OK, boys, I'm in charge of camp for the rest of the day. Barry got a terribly important letter in the mail an hour ago, and he's had to go to Bemidji. He'll be back in time for our campfire get-together."

Well, if there was anything I liked better than anything else, it was to be alone with only our gang, when it can be its own boss, even though we all liked Barry a lot and would do anything he said anytime.

"Bill's my boss," Dragonfly said.

I looked at Dragonfly and then at Big Jim and winked.

Big Jim grinned back and then said to all of us, "Let's get the camp chores done." He gave commands to different ones of us to do different things. Poetry and I had the job of burying the entrails and heads of some fish that Barry had caught and which had just been cleaned before he left. That is the best thing to do with fish heads and other parts of the fish that you aren't going to eat.

"The shovel's in Barry's tent," Big Jim said, and a minute later Poetry and I were on our way up along the shore to the burying place.

We hadn't gone far when we heard somebody coming behind us on the run, and it was Dragonfly, with an excited face, who said, "You crazy goofs! You going to dig for the treasure without letting me go along?"

"Why, hello, my man Friday!" I said pleasantly and told him what we were having to do. "Here—you carry the shovel and do the digging."

And Poetry said, "You can carry these fish insides." And with that he handed him the small pail he'd been carrying.

But Dragonfly wouldn't do that, so I let him disobey for once.

When we got to the place, we saw all kinds of little mounds of fresh dirt where other fish entrails had been buried. And then all of a sudden Poetry said, "There's fish heads scattered all over the ground here!"

I looked, and he was right. All around were old half-eaten bullheads, and the eyes and ugly noses of walleyed pike, and two or three spatulate-shaped snouts of big northern pike.

Dragonfly said, "Somebody's been digging them up—" And then he grabbed his nose just in time to stop most of what might have been several very noisy sneezes.

"I—*ker-chew!*—I smell—*ker-chew!*—s–something *d–dead.*"

Well, that was that, and I got a sinking feeling in my stomach, because right away I knew that what we'd smelled back in and around the mystery cabin was maybe something like this.

"It's raccoons," I heard a voice saying behind us and recognized it as Circus's voice. Since his pop was a hunter, Circus would know about coons' habits.

"Big Jim sent me to tell you guys to bury them *deep,* because the chipmunks and coons have been digging them all up again."

Well, we buried our stuff very deep, each one of us doing a little bit, but for some reason I wasn't feeling very happy. I was beginning to feel that all the mystery and excitement we'd been having and which had been getting more exciting every minute, was all made out of our own imagination.

"Do you suppose that map with invisible ink on it was only maybe showing somebody where a *fish cemetery* is?" Poetry asked, and I felt terribly sad inside. We all looked at each other with sad eyes and felt even sadder.

"Then Tom's dad is only up here on a fishing trip, and he's maybe rented the old cabin from somebody for a while," I said.

We went back to camp feeling dreadfully down.

After supper and when it was almost dark, it was time for Eagle Eye's bloodcurdling Indian story. We knew that since he was a Christian Indian, he would tell us a Bible story too, which is one reason why our parents had wanted us to come on this camping trip in the first place.

Every night before we tumbled into bed, we would listen to a short talk from the Bible, and then somebody would lead us in prayer. Sometimes somebody gave us a talk about what boys ought to know about themselves and God, and how God expected everybody in the world to behave themselves—things like that. Not a one of the gang was sissified enough to be ashamed of being a Christian, and, as you know, every single one of us nearly always carried his New Testament with him wherever he went.

So we started our evening campfire, which was going to be what is called an "Indian fire." It was after Eagle Eye's story that I found out about Little Tom's terribly sad heart, and I was even gladder than before that he hadn't been with us that afternoon. I think I never felt so sorry for anybody in my life as I did for red-haired Little Tom Till at the close of our campfire.

7

It was fun having our big Indian guest, Eagle Eye, whom we all knew and liked very much, take charge of our meeting. First, he showed us how to build an Indian fire. It was like this: To begin with, he made a little wigwam of some dry tinder and slender sticks and some larger sticks, all stacked up in the shape of a tepee, with the top ends overlapping each other a little. Then he had us boys drag five or six big long poles from a little shelter nearby, where there was a place for keeping wood dry.

It was interesting to watch him. Just for fun he was wearing real Indian garb, a headband filled with long, different-colored feathers, and clothes that looked like the kind I'd seen in pictures of Indians in our school library.

As soon as the wigwam fire was laid, but not started yet, he took his bow and arrow and what he called a "fire board," and in almost no time had a small fire started. It was a pretty sight to watch that little wigwam of tinder and sticks leap into flame and the reddish-yellow tongues of fire go shooting toward the sky. The smoke rose slowly and spread itself out over our camp and sort of hung there like a big, lazy bluish cloud.

Little Jim and I were sitting side by side,

and Tom Till was right across the fire from us. The ground was still wet, so we were sitting on our camp chairs. Since it was a little chilly, I had a blanket wrapped around me and had it spread out to cover Little Jim too, because he was my favorite small guy of the whole gang.

For some reason, whenever Little Jim was with me, I seemed to be a better boy—or anyway, I wished I was. It was the easiest thing in the world to think about the Bible and God and about everybody needing to be saved and things like that, when Little Jim was with us. And yet he was as much a rough-and-tumble boy as any of the rest of us. I never will forget the way he shot and killed that fierce old mother bear down along Sugar Creek—which you know about if you've read *Killer Bear*.

"Here's a good way to save labor," Eagle Eye told us as soon as our wigwam fire had burned down a little.

He picked up one of the long thick poles and dragged it to the fire and laid the end of it right across the still burning wigwam. Then he dragged up another pole and laid the end of it across the end of the first one. Pretty soon he had the ends of all the poles crisscrossed on the fire with their opposite ends stretching out in all directions like the spokes of a wagon wheel. Almost right away the big hot flames were leaping up like Circus's pop's hungry dogs leaping around a Sugar Creek tree where they've treed a coon. It was certainly a pretty sight.

"Pretty soon, when the ends of the poles are burned up, we'll push the poles in a little further," Eagle Eye said, "and you won't have to chop them in short pieces at all. When you want your fire to go out at bedtime, just pull the poles back from the fire and pour water on the ends."

I looked across at my man Friday, and he grinned back at me and said, "I'd rather have him for my boss than Robinson Crusoe himself," which was maybe half funny, I thought.

"Tomorrow night, you can use the same poles, and you don't have to chop," Eagle Eye explained.

Then Eagle Eye wrapped his blanket around him and sat down on a log and began his story. First he took out his Bible—he is a missionary, you know, to his own people.

Before he got started, though, Little Jim, who was cuddled up under my blanket, whispered, "That pretty blue smoke hanging up there—it's like the pillar of cloud it tells about in the Bible. When it hung above the camp of the people of Israel, it meant God wanted them to stay there awhile. And when it lifted itself up higher, it meant they were supposed to travel on."

I'd heard that story many a time in Sunday school or church, and I liked it a lot. I didn't understand it very well, though, not until that very second when Little Jim, who had his eyes focused on Eagle Eye as he opened his Bible and also on the blue smoke cloud, said in my ear, "I'll bet the cloud was there to show the people that God loved them and was right there to look after them and take care of them."

Imagine that little guy thinking that, but it seemed maybe he was right.

Then Eagle Eye told his story, which was a different kind of story than I'd expected. It was all about how his father had been such a good father until he learned to drink whiskey. And then one night he had gotten drunk and drove his car into a telephone pole away up at the place where the highway and the sandy road meet. "You boys notice next time you're there. There's a cross, which the Highway Commission put there, to remind people that somebody met his death there by a car accident."

Eagle Eye stopped talking a minute, and I saw him fumble under his blanket for something. It was a handkerchief, which he used to wipe a couple of quick tears from his eyes. It was the first time I'd ever seen him with tears in his eyes, and I realized that Indians were people like anyone else and could feel sad inside and love their parents the same as anybody else God had made.

Then my eyes went across the circle to where Tom Till was sitting beside Big Jim, and I saw him swallow hard as though there was a big lump in his throat. He was just staring into the fire as though he wasn't seeing it at all but was seeing something or somebody very far away. I knew that if he was imagining anything about his father, his thoughts wouldn't have to travel very far but only to an abandoned old cabin on a lake—but he didn't know that.

Then Eagle Eye brought something else from under his blanket, and the minute I saw it I realized it was going to be hard for Tom to sit still and listen. But there it was—a big whiskey bottle with pretty flowers on its very pretty label.

Eagle Eye held up the bottle in the firelight for us all to see. He said, "This is the enemy that killed my father. I found it half empty in the car where he died. This bottle is responsible for my father's broken neck and the broken windshield that cut his face beyond recognition."

Eagle Eye stopped then. He took the bottle in both of his hands, held it out and looked at it, and shook his head sadly.

While everything was quiet for a moment, with only the sound of the crackling fire and the sound of Little Jim's irregular breathing beside me, I noticed that Tom Till had both fists doubled up tight as if he was terribly mad at something or somebody.

Then Eagle Eye talked again. "The evil spirit, the Devil, paints all sin pretty, boys, but sin is bad. All sin is bad, and only Jesus can save from sin. You boys pray for my people. Too many of them are learning to drink."

Well, the story was finished, and Barry wasn't back yet to take charge of the last part of our campfire meeting, so I knew Big Jim would have to do it. It was what we called Prayer Time, and just before somebody was supposed to lead us in a prayer, the leader asked questions around the circle, in case any of us had anything or anybody we wanted prayer for.

So Big Jim took charge and started by saying he wanted us to pray for him, because someday he might want to be a missionary.

Circus was next, so he spoke up and said, "Everybody thank the Lord for saving my pop from being a drunk." The very minute he said it, I was both glad and sad and looked quick at Tom Till, who was still staring into the fire with his fists doubled up.

Dragonfly said, "Pray for my mother."

Poetry frowned, trying to think, then said, "For new mission hospitals to be built in foreign countries like Africa and other places."

It was Tom Till's turn next, but he sat with his head down and was looking at his doubled-up fists. I could see he was afraid to say a word for fear his voice would break and he'd cry.

So Big Jim skipped him, and it was Little Jim's turn. He piped up from beside me and said in his mouselike voice, "Everybody pray for Shorty Long back home."

I certainly was surprised. Shorty Long was the new tough guy who had moved into Sugar Creek territory last winter and had started coming to our school and had caused a terrible lot of trouble for the gang. But that was like Little Jim, praying for someone like that.

Next it was my turn. I'd been thinking all the time while the different requests were being made and hadn't decided yet just what to ask for. But all of a sudden I remembered something my bushy-browed, reddish-brown-mustached dad prays for when he asks the blessing at the table at our house. So I said, "Pray for all the brokenhearted people in the world." When Dad prays, he always adds, "A broken and a contrite heart, O God, You will not despise."

For a while after I said that, and thought that, I was lonesome for my folks—for my dad; and my brown-haired mother; and my neat baby sister, Charlotte Ann; and our black-and-white cat; and our kind of old house; and our big gray barn; and Dad's beehives; and our potato patch.

Also I wished, for just a second, that I could stand and take one big happy look at Sugar Creek itself, at the weedy riffle just below the old swimming hole, and the leaning linden tree above the spring, and Bumblebee Hill, where we'd had first met Tom Till and his big brother, Bob. That was where we'd had a fight, and I licked Tom, and at the bottom of that hill we had run *ker-smack* into the angry mother bear and her cub. And to save himself and all of us, Little Jim had shot her.

Well, that was all our prayer requests, except Little Tom's, and Big Jim was going to be courteous enough not to ask him, so he wouldn't be embarrassed. But then Tom spoke up and said, "Pray for my daddy, that he'll come home again and will get a good job."

Then he picked up a stick that was in front of him and reached out and shoved the end of it into the fire, where it sent up a lot of pretty yellow sparks toward the blue smoke cloud up there.

For some reason a thought flashed into my mind as if somebody had turned on a light in my head, and it was that Little Tom's request was already on its way up to God, just as the sparks had shot up toward the sky. I felt that someday God was going to answer and give him a good daddy just like Circus's pop was after he was saved. And Tom's mother would be happy, and the whole family could go to church together. They would have enough to eat, and better clothes to wear, and everything.

It certainly didn't look as if the answer was going to come very soon, though—not after John Till was described by a radio announcer as maybe the one who had helped the kidnapper. Right now maybe John Till knew where the ransom money was buried, if it was. And if he got caught, I thought, he'd have to go to jail, and this time maybe he'd have to stay a terribly long time—years and years.

Well, Eagle Eye gathered up all our requests, like a boy gathering up an armload of wood, and took them to God in some very nice friendly words, handing them to Him to look over and to answer as soon as He could and in the best way.

I felt good inside just watching Eagle Eye pray, although I shut my eyes *almost* right away.

First, he took off his big Indian hat, and I noticed he had an ordinary haircut. He left his blanket wrapped around him, though, and shut his eyes and just stood there with his brown face lit up by the fire, and he talked to the heavenly Father as though they were good friends.

Then the meeting broke up, and pretty soon it was time for us to go to bed.

All of us were as noisy as usual at bedtime except Tom, and I noticed he still had a sad expression on his face. I had a chance to talk with him alone a minute, just before we went to our separate tents. I walked with him to the end of the dock, where we stood looking out over the shimmering waves of the lake under the half-moon that was shining on it, and I said, "'S'matter, Tom? Something the matter?"

He stood there, not saying a word.

I said, "You're one of my best friends, Tom."

Then he answered me very sadly. "The mail boat brought a letter from Mother, and she's worried about Dad. He's gone again, and nobody knows where he is."

I didn't know what to say for a moment, so I just stood beside him, thinking and feeling sorry for him, wishing his dad was saved like Circus's pop and that the Till family would all be Christians.

I don't know why I thought what I did just then, but it was something I'd heard Old Man Paddler say once. He said, "A lot of husbands are murdering their wives a little at a time. Someday a lot of mean husbands are going to look down into the coffins at their wives' funerals and realize that, by not being kind to them, their wives died ten years sooner than they should have—and that's the same as murder."

In that way, old John Till was a murderer too, I thought, as well as an alcoholic. And it made me feel even more sorry for the great little red-haired, freckled-faced guy who stood beside me.

Tom had his back to me. Both of his hands were clasped around the flagpole at the end of the dock, and he was just weaving backward and forward and sideways as though he was nervous.

"Don't worry, Tom," I said. "You've got a lot of friends, and my mother thinks your mother is great."

Right then I got the surprise of my life. I hadn't realized that this little guy liked his wicked father a lot too. He said, "There are a lot of crosses all over the country like the one Eagle Eye told us about, just like the one they put up for his Indian daddy—"

Then Little Tom stopped talking, and I heard him sniffle, and I knew it wasn't because of the breeze from the lake or because he was allergic to anything. He *liked* his daddy and didn't want him to get drunk and have a car accident and get killed.

I felt terribly sad, but at the same time a sort of wonderful feeling came bubbling up inside of me. I liked that little guy so much it actually hurt inside my heart.

I reached out the way my dad does to me sometimes, and before I knew I was going to do it I'd given him the same kind of a half hug Dad gives me. I said, "Listen, Tom. I think God's going to answer Eagle Eye's prayer for you."

Then I was bashful as anything and just stood there beside him while he kept on weaving back and forth with his hands still on the flagpole. Neither one of us said a word; and the waves of the lake made a friendly sound, lapping against the dock posts and washing against the sandy shore.

Well, the gang started yelling from the tents for us to hurry and come to bed, so Tom and I started back toward the Indian fire. The fire was still alive, although the flames were kind of lazy, and the big blue cloud of smoke that had been hanging above our camp, mixed with the night sky, seemed to be gone.

Tom and I stopped beside the fire a minute and looked down into it. Then just as he'd done before, he picked up a stick and shoved it into the coals, and a whole lot of sparks came out and shot toward the sky.

"Hey, you—Bill," Big Jim called to me from his tent, "it's your turn to put out the fire. The water pail is here in Barry's tent—"

Every night we had to pour water on our campfires so that there wouldn't be any danger of them suddenly coming to life in a wind and starting a forest fire.

It didn't take me long to get the pail, dip up some water from the lake, and pour it on that fire till there wasn't even one tiny spark visible.

Little Jim came out and went along with me as I made two or three trips from the fire to the lake and back.

"There's something I want to ask you," he said to me just as I was about to leave him at his tent. He had been sleeping in Big Jim's tent with Tom Till and Barry Boyland. The rest of us—in fact, the whole *Robinson Crusoe* gang—slept in the other tent. It was my two goats and my man Friday and me.

"What?" I said.

"Can I play *Robinson Crusoe* with you tomorrow?"

I was dumbfounded. "What?" I said. "Who told you about—about our game?"

"I just guessed it," he said, "when Dragonfly said you walked on his neck, and he was a native boy, and that they'd been trying to make soup out of him."

I wouldn't promise him, because I wasn't sure what my man Friday and my two goats would think of the idea. But later when my goats and my man Friday and I were alone in our tent, we talked it over.

Friday said, "Let's let him—and he can be *my* slave."

Poetry spoke up from his sleeping bag beside me and said, "Let's let him, because he didn't get to help us find the little Ostberg girl and he wasn't even with us when we caught the kidnapper in the Indian cemetery!"

So that was that. We wouldn't take Tom Till along though. We didn't want him to know his daddy was up here and that he might be mixed up with the kidnapping mystery. Also, for some reason it didn't seem right to have Big Jim come along and be our leader, when Robinson Crusoe had to be the leader himself.

Boy oh boy! I could hardly wait till tomorrow!

For a long time I lay awake in our dark tent, smelling the smell of mosquito lotion and hearing the noise of Dragonfly's snoring and the regular breathing of Poetry and Circus. I was thinking a lot of things. I hadn't said my prayers yet, and I was already in my sleeping bag with the zipper zipped up, although I'd prayed with the rest of the gang around the fire when Eagle Eye prayed out loud for all of us.

But it seemed it had been a dangerous day, as well as a very wonderful one, and God had taken good care of all of us, and I ought to tell Him so. Of course, I could just talk to Him without kneeling, the way I sometimes do, but this seemed extra important.

So very quietly I zipped open my sleeping bag, squirmed myself into a kneeling position, and while a mosquito sang in my right ear without stinging me, because the ear had mosquito repellent on it, I said a few extra special words to God. I wound up by saying, "And please don't let John Till murder Little Tom's mother.

Please save him as quick as You can, and if there is anything I can do to help You, let me know, and I'll try to do it."

A little later, while I was lying warm and cozy in my bag, listening to Dragonfly's crooked nose snoring away like a handsaw cutting through a board, it seemed there was kind of a warm secret between God and me and that it might not be very long until Tom would have a new daddy. Then I dozed off into sleep, and right away, it seemed, I was mixed up in the craziest dream I ever was mixed up in.

My dream was about John Till, and it seemed he was all tangled up in the kidnapping mystery. John had a bottle of whiskey in one hand and was standing beside the sink in the old cabin, pouring the whiskey over a stringer of fish. He kept on pouring and pouring. In fact, the whiskey bottle sort of faded out of the dream, and John was pumping the old iron pitcher pump, which, quick as an eyewink was standing at the end of the board walk in our backyard at Sugar Creek. Whiskey instead of water was coming in big belches out of the pitcher's mouth and was splashing down over the fish, which were in our water tank, where our cows and horses drank.

All of a sudden I noticed that the stringer of fish had all changed, and there wasn't a walleye or a northern pike among them, but only big, dark brown, ugly bullheads. And they weren't on the stringer anymore but were swimming around and playing and acting lively in our water tank filled with whiskey. Poetry, who was standing beside me in my dream, said in my ear, "Look, Bill—the whiskey's changed all the fish into bullheads." It was a silly dream.

Right that second I felt something touching me in the ribs. I forced my stubborn eyes open a little but couldn't see much because it was very dark in our tent. But I did see the shadow of someone leaning over me, and after such a crazy dream I was scared of who it might be.

Then I heard Poetry's husky whisper right close to my face saying, "Hey, Bill!"

"What?" I whispered up at him. My mind was all tangled up with mixed-up ideas.

Poetry's whisper back in my ear was, "Let's take a look at the invisible-ink map. I just dreamed there was another line running off in a different direction. Let's hold a hot flashlight down real close to it and see if there is."

I didn't want to wake up—rather, I *did* want to go back to sleep again—but Poetry kept on whispering excitedly about his dream. So I reached over to my shirt, which I had hung on my camp chair close by, and ran my hand into the pocket where I'd kept the map. Well, I hadn't any sooner got my hand inside than a very scared feeling woke me up quick.

"Hey!" I whispered to Poetry. "It's not in my pocket!"

8

S ure it is," Poetry said. "It's got to be!"

"But it's not!" I said, more wide awake than I usually am when I am wide awake. I must have made a lot of excited noise because Dragonfly stopped snoring, sneezed a couple of times, and wanted to know what was going on and why.

"Nothing," my roly-poly goat said to him. "We're just looking for something."

"Well, look with your *eyes* instead of your *voices*," Dragonfly said. "I'm allergic to—*ker-chew!*—to—*ker-chew!*—to *noise!*"

"It's your own snoring that woke you up," Poetry said to my man Friday. "Now go back to sleep."

I certainly felt strange. "Somebody's *stolen* it," I said to Poetry. I was running my hands frantically through all the pockets of my trousers and shirt and all the other clothes I'd had on during the day.

We flashed the flashlight all around the tent and into every corner where the envelope might have fallen out of one of my pockets.

"We've *got* to find it," Poetry said. "Where do you suppose you lost it?"

"*Lost* it! Somebody's sneaked in here and stolen it!"

"Hey!" Poetry said, as though he had thought of a bright idea. "When do you remember looking at it last?"

My thoughts galloped back over the evening and then the afternoon, and I couldn't remember.

"What pocket did you have it in last?" he asked.

I thought and said, "Why, my shirt pocket where I keep my New Testament. I put it there when I—"

And then I stopped talking and gasped. I'd thought of something. "Maybe we—maybe it dropped out of my pocket back there in the cabin when we were climbing out of the window."

Then Poetry said, "Yeah, or maybe you left it out on the front porch, and that's why John Till didn't come back to try to stop us. Maybe he found it on the floor out there and picked it up—if it was what he'd been looking for."

My acrobatic goat came to life then. He groaned and turned over and tried to go back to sleep.

Poetry was more excited than I was. He said, "Bill Collins, we've *got* to find that map, and I don't think we lost it around here anywhere."

"Let's all go back to sleep," my man Friday said.

"Go ahead. Who's stopping you?" I said.

I scrambled into my clothes, while Poetry did the same thing, each of us knowing what the other one of us wanted to do. In less time than it takes to tell, we had on enough clothes so we wouldn't get cold when we stepped outside into the chilly night, as nights are up North even in the summertime.

We had our two flashlights and were soon looking around the outside of our tent, sneaking along as quietly as we could so as not to wake up any of the rest of the gang in the other tent. We flashed our flashlights on and off all around the circle where we had been sitting at the campfire service. But there was no sign of any envelope there. Then we looked all around the lean-to where we had gotten the dry logs for Eagle Eye's Indian fire. But we still didn't find anything.

So Poetry and I followed the path up the shore to the fish cemetery and looked all around where we had been digging to bury the fish heads and entrails.

"Maybe it fell out of your pocket when you were digging here," he said.

But there wasn't a sign of what we were looking for there, either. It was just like looking for a needle in a haystack when there wasn't any needle to look for.

"Will you *ever!*" Poetry exclaimed, tossing his light all around in a circle at the newly made fish graves. "The coons have already been here."

I could see they had. I flashed my light from place to place and off into the woods in a big circle and up into the trees. But I didn't see a thing that looked like bright shining eyes or pretty gray fur or a furry tail with black rings around it, which is the kind of tails ring-tailed coons have.

From the fish cemetery we went out to the end of the dock and back, then to our tent again. When we stopped in front of the closed flap we listened, but my man Friday and my acrobatic goat were as quiet as mice, so we decided they were asleep.

"Do you know what?" Poetry said, and I said, "What?" and he said, "I think we'd better go back up along the trail where we were this afternoon to see if maybe we dropped it along there somewhere."

I couldn't imagine being able to find it at night even if it was there. Besides, I still had the notion—in fact, a very creepy feeling inside of me—that somebody must've sneaked into our tent while we were asleep and stolen it out of my pocket.

"Well," Poetry said, "when did you last *look* at it? When did you last have it out of your pocket? Where were you when you *last* saw it?"

And I must confess that the last time I had seen the envelope was when we were still at the cabin. I had shoved it into my shirt pocket right beside where I kept my New Testament.

When I told Poetry that, he said, "OK, then, when did you last have your New Testament out of your pocket?"

Well, I gasped out loud when he said that, for I remembered that I'd had my New Testa-

95

ment out of my pocket when I was on the porch of the old cabin where John Till was. I'd been holding it in my hand while I was looking out across the very pretty, terribly stormy lake.

"You mean you haven't looked at it since then?" Poetry asked me, astonished, and I said, "No."

I was astonished at myself, but then of course we'd all decided not to tell the rest of the gang but to keep the map secret for a while. That explained why I hadn't taken it out of my pocket. Eagle Eye hadn't asked us to read any verses out of the Bible, so I hadn't even thought of opening my New Testament. If I had, I would no doubt have noticed that the envelope was missing.

"OK, come on," Poetry said. "Let's get going," which we did, hurrying as fast as we could through the wet grass and along the path that was bordered by the still wet bushes, although the late afternoon sun had dried things off quite a bit.

Down the shore we went, past the boat-house, up the steep hill, and along the sandy road, shining our flashlights on and off as we went. I carried with me a stout stick, just in case we ran into anything or anybody that might need to be socked in order to save our lives.

As we hurried along in the moonlight, I was glad there weren't supposed to be any bears up here and that where we were camping there weren't supposed to be any wild animals at all except deer, polecats, raccoons, chipmunks, and maybe a few other more or less friendly wild animals—all of which would be half scared to death if they saw us hurrying past carrying flashlights.

When we came to the place where we had found the little Ostberg girl, we flashed our lights on the tree Circus had climbed and all around where my acrobatic goat's firecracker had started the little fire that we had put out in a hurry. I even went over and picked up the empty prune can, which the cannibals had left and which the goats hadn't eaten, and looked inside, knowing, of course, that the envelope wasn't *there*.

"We'd better follow the trail of broken twigs down to John Till's cabin," Poetry said. "Maybe it fell out of your pocket down there some place."

I was scared to get anywhere near John Till, remembering his big hunting knife, but I kept thinking all the time what I had been thinking before, which was, *What if John Till has found the map and has gone to dig for the treasure? If the police find him with it in his possession, the newspapers will print the story, and the Sugar Creek Gang will get a black eye all over the country. On top of that, Little Tom Till will be ashamed to come to Sunday school or even to school.* Besides, if we could save old John Till from having to go to jail, he might not ever have to go again.

I knew that if he had to go once more, having been in jail a good many times in his life, he'd maybe have to stay in ten or fifteen years this time. So if we could stop him from finding the ransom money, it'd be a good idea. Besides, the money was supposed to be used for a hospital on a foreign missionary field, which made it seem important that we find it ourselves.

We came to the first broken branch. And even as scared as Poetry and I were, we zipped on, using our flashlights till we came to the next, and the next. In a little while we were at the top of the hill and looking down at the moonlight on the lake. Between us and the lake was the cabin where we had had all our excitement in the afternoon.

"Look at that!" Poetry said. "There's smoke coming out of the chimney!" And there was. We could see it in the moonlight, rising slowly from the brick chimney top and spreading itself out into a large lazy cloud just like the one Little Jim had whispered to me about—the one that had been hanging above our heads and had reminded him of the one that had been above the camp of the people in the Bible, meaning that God was right there looking after them and loving them and protecting them.

For a minute, right in the middle of all that excitement I got a warm feeling in my heart that God was right there with Poetry and me and that He loved us and was looking after us, and also that we were doing the right thing.

"Look!" I whispered, holding onto Poetry's arm so tight he said, "Not so tight. I *am* looking!"

Through one of the windows, we could see a flickering fire in the fireplace. From where we were, we could see past the kitchen window but couldn't see *into* it. Then I felt my hair rising right up under my cap, for there was the shadow of a man climbing out that window. A flashlight went on and off real quick.

"*Sh!*" Poetry said, because I had gasped. "He's coming this way."

He was, but only for a few feet till he got to the corner of the cabin. Then he would turn and follow the cement walk that led along the side of the house and down the slope to the dock.

I could hardly believe my ears, but I had to. The man was whistling a tune, and it was "Old Black Joe," which we sometimes sang out of a songbook at Sugar Creek School. We also used different words to it in our church, which were:

Once I was lost and way down deep in sin,
Once was a slave to passions fierce within.
Once was afraid to trust a loving God,
But now my sins are washed away in Jesus'
    blood.

I knew John Till wouldn't be thinking of *those* words when he whistled but would be thinking of the "Old Black Joe" ones.

At the corner he came out into the moonlight, where we saw him as clear as anything. He had on a pair of rubber boots, a fishing pole in one hand, and a big stringer of fish, which looked like the very same stringer he had in the sink in the afternoon.

"He's going out to clean his fish," Poetry said.

"And he's got a shovel to bury the insides with," I said, noticing it for the first time.

We stood glued to our tracks and holding onto each other, wondering, *What on earth!* We hardly dared move or breathe because the cement walk came in our direction before it turned to make its long half circle down to the dock and the lake.

"Or maybe he's going down to put his fish in a live box," Poetry said, which is what fishermen sometimes do with the fish they've caught, especially if they don't want to clean and eat them right away. They keep them alive in what is called a "live box" down at the lake near their dock.

"But those fish would have been dead by now," I said. "They wouldn't stay alive in that sink all this time—not with all that whiskey all over them."

And Poetry said, "What whiskey all over what, where?"

Then I remembered that I had only dreamed about the whiskey coming out of the pump and filling the sink. I felt foolish, but that dream had seemed so real that it was just as if it had actually happened.

John Till's whistle sounded farther and farther away as he turned the corner and went down the hill, and pretty soon we saw him coming out in the moonlight on the dock away down at the lake.

"There's a boat!" Poetry whispered. "He's getting into a boat," which is what John was doing.

In the next minute and a half, while we stood up there with our teeth chattering, partly because it was a cold and damp night and partly because we were scared, we saw the flash of an oar blade in the moonlight. A little later the boat was shoved out from the dock, and we saw John Till rowing along the shore.

Well, I didn't know what was going to happen next, or whether anything would, because it seemed like everything that could possibly happen had already happened.

But Poetry was as brave as anything. Certainly he was braver than I was right at that minute, or else we decided to do what we decided to do in spite of being afraid.

"Let's go in the cabin and look around and see if we can find the map," Poetry said.

The very minute John Till's boat disappeared around the bend of the shore, we sneaked down the hill to the kitchen window. We could see the flames leaping up in the fireplace in the main room. In a flash Poetry had the window up, and we had climbed in. We could smell fish and also a sort of a dead smell in the cabin, but the cabin was warm and cozy with the fire going.

We took a quick look in the bedroom, and there was the roll-away bed all nicely opened out with blankets on it and ready for somebody to use.

We shone our lights in quick circles all over the floor, thinking maybe John Till might not have known there was an envelope, which we might have dropped here. Then we went out onto the front porch and looked very carefully in the direction his boat had gone, to be sure he was really around the bend and couldn't see our lights.

"Here's the whiskey bottle, standing just where it was," Poetry said. "And it's still just as half full as it was!"

I looked and could hardly believe my eyes, but it was true.

"It must have had water in it instead of whiskey," Poetry said, "or John Till would have drunk it up the very minute he laid his eyes on it."

I put my nose close to the top of the bottle and smelled, but it smelled just like whiskey, which is an even worse smell than something that has been dead for a week.

I looked down at the place where I had been standing that afternoon when I'd pulled the New Testament out of my pocket—to see if the envelope with the map in it was there, and it wasn't. Then we turned and walked back toward the door that led into the main room.

When I got to the place where the mirror was on the wall, I looked in it just to have a look at myself. Then I looked past my face and away out onto the very pretty lake, shimmering like silver in the moonlight. Even though I didn't have time to think about how pretty it was, I remembered the happy feeling I'd had in my heart in the afternoon.

And while Poetry and I were going through the main room, past the fireplace and into the kitchen, and were climbing out of the window to go back to camp, I thought that God could make just as pretty a moonlit night as He could a thunderstorm. In spite of the fact that I was all tangled up in a very interesting and exciting adventure, I couldn't help but be glad that I was on God's side and that He could count on me to be a friend of His anytime He needed me.

We didn't have any trouble following our broken twig trail to the place where it turned off in another direction. There we stopped, and Poetry said, "I wish we could follow this trail of broken branches tonight and not wait till tomorrow. It might be too late tomorrow. Do you know that it goes in the same direction John Till's boat was going?"

"What of it?" I said. My teeth were still chattering, and I was cold and wet and tired and wished I was back in camp, snuggled down in my nice, warm, cozy sleeping bag. "We'd get lost in less than three minutes," I said to Poetry, "and then what would we do?"

"It's as easy as pie not to get lost," he said. "You stay right here with your flashlight, and I'll go in the direction the broken twigs point until I find the next one. Then you go to the *next* one, and we can keep doing that from one to another until we get there."

"Get where?" I asked.

"Where the treasure is buried," he said with an impatient voice.

"But we haven't anything to dig with," I said in a voice just as impatient.

We stood for a little while arguing with each other as to what to do and whether to do it.

"Let's try it anyway!" Poetry said. "You stay here till I go and see if I can find the next broken branch. Keep your flashlight turned off as much as you can—to save the battery," he ordered.

And for some reason, I, Robinson Crusoe, gave up and let my roly-poly goat be the leader.

I watched him go in a sort of zigzag style in the general direction the broken twigs pointed. I could hear him swishing around up ahead of me. It felt awfully spooky there in that dark woods with my light turned off and only little patches of moonlight around me, coming through the leaves and pine needles of the trees overhead.

After about four minutes, Poetry's half-bass and half-soprano voice called to me, saying, "Turn on your flashlight, so I can find out where I am!"

I turned on my light and shot its long beam in the direction from which I had heard his voice.

He shone his toward me. Then his half-worried voice called, "Is your broken twig pointing toward me?"

"No!" I said. "You're off in a different direction. Why don't we get out of here and go home? I don't think we can follow any trail tonight."

I knew it would have been easy if we had followed the trail in the daytime and had known what kind of broken branches to look for and how far apart they were.

Poetry didn't like to give up, so when he got back to where I was, he wanted to start out again.

But I said, "What if we would get lost out there somewhere?"

"We'd just follow the trail back again," he said, but his voice sounded as if he had already given up.

We decided to go back to camp and get some sleep, and tomorrow we would come back in broad daylight and be able to see where we were going.

9

We hurried back to camp as quickly as we could, sneaked into our tent where my acrobatic goat and my man Friday were sleeping, and started undressing and getting into our pajamas. I felt pretty sad because the map was gone, but there wasn't anything we could do till morning.

We kept our flashlights turned off so as not to wake up the other two guys. We could see a little because of the moonlight that was pouring down on the top of our tent.

"Where you guys been?" my man Friday said to me from behind.

His voice scared me because I'd thought he was asleep.

"We've been out looking for the invisible-ink map," my roly-poly goat answered for me. "Either somebody stole it out of Robinson Crusoe's shirt pocket, or we lost it back on the trail somewhere this afternoon."

"Oh, is that where you've been?" my man Friday said. "Why didn't you tell me? I've got it here under my pillow. I was afraid somebody would steal it, so I took it out of Crusoe's pocket and hid it here."

"What!" I said fiercely, more disgusted with him than I had been for a long time. I made a dive for him, so half mad I could have beaten him up.

"Don't hurt me!" he cried, turning his face and burying it in his pillow. The minute he did it, his nose objected by making him sneeze. "Your man Friday—*ker-chew!*—has to look after you, doesn't he?"

Well, that was that. Poetry and I were so tired and so sleepy that we didn't feel like telling Dragonfly and Circus what we had seen going on up at the old cabin.

I got the map away from Dragonfly and put it down inside my sleeping bag with me, next to my chest, happy that it wasn't lost and feeling cozy and warm and glad to have a warm bed to sleep in.

And the next thing I knew it was morning.

Our mystery was still unsolved, but it was a wonderful sunshiny day with blue sky, and the lake was as smooth as a pane of blue glass.

Barry still hadn't come back, so Big Jim was in charge of us till noon.

Little Tom Till was our main problem. I'd promised to let Little Jim play *Robinson Crusoe* with us today, but what to do about Tom Till? I hated to tell him his daddy was up here in the north woods and that the police were looking for him.

"How'll we get away without taking Big Jim and Little Tom Till and without having them ask all kinds of questions?" I asked Poetry.

He grinned and said, "It's as easy as pie. The rest of you just sneak away without anyone noticing you. And I'll leave this note on Big Jim's tent pole."

He had a note already written. It was in poetry, and it said:

Please, Big Jim and Little Tom Till,
Do not worry, for we will
All be back in time for lunch—
We are following a hunch.
Robinson Crusoe, his man Friday,
And his three goats

It was an easy way for us to get away without having to explain where we were going and why.

In only a little while we were gone, following the sandy road toward the place where, the week before, Poetry and I had found the Ostberg girl. We all explained some of the mystery to Little Jim as we went along.

My man Friday was carrying the shovel we were going to dig up the money with, and Little Jim was carrying his stick and an empty gunnysack he'd found.

"What's the gunnysack for?" Dragonfly asked him.

And Little Jim said, "We're going after buried treasure, aren't we?"

When we came to the place where we'd built the imaginary fire with which to cook Dragonfly, Little Jim got the cutest grin on his face and said, "Here's where *I* come in. Somebody shoot me quick, so I can turn into a goat."

"*Bang!*" I said, pointing my finger at him. "Now you're dead."

Little Jim plopped himself down on the ground, then jumped up and said, "Now I'm a goat." He began to sniff at my hand like a good goat.

He surely was a great guy and had a good imagination, I thought. But somehow our game had turned from innocent fun to a very serious and maybe dangerous game.

We followed our broken-twig trail to where it branched off in two directions—one trail going toward the cabin where we'd seen John Till twice, and the other going toward where the ransom money was buried—we hoped.

"Which way first?" my man Friday asked. Then he got a screwed-up expression on his face, sniffed, and said, "There's that *deadish* smell again."

And it was. I turned my nose in different directions to find out which way it was coming from. But I couldn't tell for sure.

"Come on!" my acrobatic goat said. "Let's get going." And he and my roly-poly goat started down the trail we hadn't followed yet.

There was no use for me to get mad that they didn't wait for my orders before going ahead, so I said, "Sure, that's what I say."

Away we all went, Little Jim carrying his stick, wearing a grin and also a very serious expression on his smallish face. He held his stick as if he was ready to sock anything that might need socking.

It was fun following the trail. Yet, as we moved along from one broken twig to another and to another, I was remembering what a dangerous surprise we had found yesterday when we came to the end of that other trail.

It certainly wasn't a straight trail. It kept zigzagging in different directions, and it seemed from the direction of the sun that it was working around toward the lake again. Soon we came to a hill and looked down, and there was the lake ahead of us. At the foot of the hill we could see through the heavy undergrowth a building of some kind. The broken wild plum twig where we were standing pointed straight toward the old building.

We stood surprised. I had expected to find a little mound of some kind, or some markings on a tree, or something else, but certainly not an oldish building.

We got out the invisible-ink map and studied it. There wasn't anything on it that looked like a house.

"It's an old icehouse," Poetry said.

And so it seemed to be, a dilapidated, unpainted log icehouse. An icehouse is a building where people up in the lake country stored ice in the wintertime, so that in the hot summer they could have plenty of ice for their iceboxes.

"Our hot trail suddenly turned cold," my roly-poly goat said, trying to be funny and not being very.

It certainly wasn't what I'd expected to find.

"OK," Little Jim said, "let's go down and start digging."

"In an icehouse?" my man Friday said, astonished. "You wouldn't expect to find any buried treasure in a thousand blocks of ice!"

"Why not?" Poetry said. "Most icehouses have as much sawdust in them as they do ice. The money's maybe buried in there in the sawdust."

Well, that seemed to make sense, so we circled around and came up to the icehouse on the side where there was the most shrubbery and where we'd be the least likely to be seen in case anybody was watching.

We stopped about twenty feet from the place and listened but didn't hear a thing. And then I got a sort of feverish feeling in my mind. I felt that maybe we were actually going to find the ransom money—the whole $25,000 in ten and twenty and fifty dollar bills. The mystery of playing *Robinson Crusoe* seemed to be an honest-to-goodness reality! I felt mysterious and afraid and brave all at the same time.

"All right, come on, you three goats. Come on, Friday," I said, all of a sudden waking up to the fact that I was supposed to be the leader. "Let's go in and dig."

The entrance was on the side away from the lake. The very old heavy door stood wide open on its rusty hinges, but there were short boards nailed across the entrance like the kind some people use to board up the entrance to the coal bin in their basement.

I looked over the top of the highest board, which was just about as high as my chin, and didn't see a thing inside except sawdust.

Quickly we all scrambled up and were inside the icehouse, which didn't have any windows and was only one big room, maybe twenty feet square. It seemed a little like the haymow in our barn at Sugar Creek, except that instead of having nice alfalfa hay in it, it had sawdust. Down underneath, I knew there were scores of big blocks of ice that somebody had cut out of the lake in the wintertime and had stored away here for summer use.

The old icehouse was also about the same shape as the woodshed beside the Sugar Creek schoolhouse, where we had had many a gang meeting.

About the only light that came in was from the door, although there was a small crack between two logs on the side next to the lake. It took a short while for our eyes to get accustomed to the dimness. And then I couldn't see anything but sawdust.

"Hey," Poetry said all of a sudden from the other side, where he had gone to look around. "It looks like the sawdust has been disturbed over here—like somebody had been digging here lately."

You can imagine how we felt. I could just see in my mind's eye Little Jim's gunnysack stuffed with money and all of us coming grinning happily back into camp, with Big Jim and Little Tom Till and maybe Barry Boyland looking at us with astonished eyes. I could imagine what *The Sugar Creek Times* would print about us and also how happy the Ostberg girl's dad and mom would be, so I said, "OK, Friday, give me the shovel."

"Me dig," Dragonfly said, "me white man's slave." With that he scrambled across to where Poetry was.

But Poetry hadn't waited for him. He was already down on his knees, digging with his bare hands, which is a good way to dig in sawdust.

Then all of us were down on our knees, digging as fast as we could. Little Jim was using his stick to help him, and I was using the shovel, which I'd taken away from Dragonfly, to move aside the pile of sawdust that I was digging out of my hole.

My roly-poly goat spoke up then and said, "D'you guys know that Minnesota is called the Gopher State?"

Pretty soon my shovel struck something hard, and I felt a thrill go through me. I said, "I've struck something! I've found it!" I was expecting it to be a box or a small trunk or maybe a fishing tackle box like the kind the kidnapper had had the night we caught him. And you know about that if you've read *The Indian Cemetery*.

Almost before I had the words out of my excited mouth, there was a mad scramble of boys' feet swishing through the sawdust from different directions. In seconds, most of the rest of them were all around me looking down into my hole to see what I had found.

I pushed the shovel in and out a few times, but it didn't sound as if it was striking a tin box or a trunk or anything like that.

"Listen!" I said, which we all did, but I couldn't tell what the noise sounded like.

"Let me get it out for you!" my acrobatic goat said.

I let him run his long right arm down into the hole.

Circus scooped out several handfuls of sawdust and then let out a disappointed sniff. "You've struck *ice*, Robinson Crusoe! This is an icehouse!"

I put my own hand down in the hole, and my fingers touched something cold. I also pulled out a small piece of ice that my shovel had chipped off.

"Anybody else strike ice?" I asked. And then I noticed Little Jim over in a corner, prying at something with his stick. His tongue was between his teeth the way he has it sometimes when he's working at something or other. He had a happy grin on his face also, which I could see because he was facing the opening where the light was coming in.

"What you got there, Little Jim?" I asked my blue-eyed goat.

He said, "I don't know. It's all covered with sawdust."

Almost before he'd said that, I saw two great big round glassy eyes, a very large snout, and a longish body that looked like a small log of fireplace wood.

Poetry saw it at the same time I did, but he thought quicker and exclaimed, "Hey, gang! Little Jim's dug up a terribly big northern pike!"

Quickly we started to help him get it out of the hole, although what we wanted to get it out for, I didn't know. That buried fish could mean only one thing. Somebody had caught it in the lake and had dug down here in the sawdust till he reached the ice and had laid the fish down on it and covered it up so it would keep cold and wouldn't spoil the way fish do almost right away in warm weather.

"Hey!" Dragonfly cried. "I've found *another* fish over here!"

We all looked at each other, and I felt as though the bottom of my life had fallen out. Almost before I had thought the next sad, disappointed thought, I'd said it to the rest of the gang. "So this is what our mysterious map brought us to. We should have known anybody wouldn't be dumb enough to leave a map right out in plain sight for anybody to find, if it showed where to dig for any buried *treasure!*"

There certainly wasn't anything unusual about digging up fish in an icehouse. We'd buried some ourselves in the icehouse at our camp when we'd been up here last year. Then, a week later when we'd been ready to go home,

115

we'd dug them up and packed them with sawdust and ice in a keg and taken them back to Sugar Creek.

So that was that. *We might as well go home,* I thought and said so. "Let's get out of here and go home. And keep still to everybody about what fools we've all been and—"

But Poetry interrupted me by saying, "We'll have to bury them again, or they'll spoil, and John Till will be madder than a hornet!"

"What?" I said and then remembered. We weren't very far from John Till's cabin—and we'd seen him coming this very direction last night in a boat—and one of his fish had been about the size of the one Little Jim had just dug up.

Thinking about John Till again made me decide it was time for us to get out of there in a hurry. So I started to dig fast with the shovel to make Little Jim's hole deep enough and long enough all the way down so we could lay the big northern pike's whole length on the ice before covering it up.

"You bury yours again too," I said to Dragonfly, and he started to dig his hole again, working as fast as he could.

Poetry, who was on his knees beside me, said, "Did you ever see such a fat-stomached northern pike in your life?"

I stopped digging and looked at it and decided I never had, except one I'd seen dead lying on a sandy beach once. The flies had been on that one, and it was bloated. But this one wasn't bloated. It was like it had been caught only maybe yesterday.

In a little while I had the long sawdust grave ready to lay the first corpse in it, when Poetry said to me in a whisper, "*Bill*—feel here, will you? There's something weird about this fish's stomach!"

The very excited sound of his whisper went clear through me and made me think that maybe he'd discovered something terribly important. I felt where he was feeling on the sides and stomach of the extralarge northern pike, which, even while I was doing it, I thought was about the same size as the one I'd seen in the sink in the cabin where John Till had been pumping water yesterday.

I could tell that there was something inside the fish that wasn't a part of him.

"Look!" Poetry whispered again, using his pudgy right hand to wipe the sawdust from the pike's stomach. "Here's a place where it's been sliced open and sewed up again! What do you s'pose it's got in it?"

Well, you can guess what I was supposing. I was remembering that yesterday in the old cabin I'd seen a northern the same size as this one and that John Till had a big hunting knife in his hand like the kind Barry uses to clean fish. Also I remembered that we'd seen John Till get into a boat with a stringer of big fish, right in the middle of last night, and row up the lake in this direction.

Dragonfly must have been listening to Poetry

and me instead of burying his fish as I'd ordered him, because he said, "This one's been cut open and sewed up again, too."

You can guess that we were an excited gang of treasure hunters. Of course, we didn't know we'd found anything for sure, but it certainly looked as if we had. It wouldn't take any more than a jiffy and three-fourths to find out.

Poetry took out his knife, which was an official Boy Scout knife. It had a heavy cutting blade, a screwdriver, a bottle and can opener, and a punch blade. He opened the sharp cutting blade and carefully sliced through the heavy string the fish was sewed up with, and right in front of our eyes—all the rest of the gang was gathered around—Poetry pulled out a package of something wrapped in the same kind of waterproof oil paper my mother has in our kitchen at home.

In another second we had unwrapped the package, and what to my wondering eyes should appear but a packet of money that looked like dozens and dozens of twenty dollar bills.

If I could have been somebody else standing close by and looking down at me, I'll bet I'd have seen my eyes almost bulge out of their sockets with surprise and wonder and excitement.

"We've found it, gang!" I said to us, and I knew we had.

Dragonfly piped up and said, "I'll bet there's a dozen other big fish buried here with money in 'em."

It was a wonderful feeling. First we'd found the invisible-ink map, and then the trail of broken twigs, and now we'd found the money itself. Boy oh boy oh boy! It was too good to be true!

"Now we know what the deadish smell was," Dragonfly said.

But Little Jim said, "What deadish smell?"

Dragonfly answered, "John Till took the fish's insides out while he was in the cabin and maybe, instead of burying them, just threw them outside somewhere," which I thought was pretty sensible for Dragonfly to figure out.

But we couldn't just stay there and be like King Midas and count our money. We ought to get back to camp and tell the gang and Barry and let the whole world know what we'd found.

"Let's get all of it dug up and take it away before John Till finds out we discovered his hiding place," Poetry said.

"But there might be a *dozen* other fish with money in them," I said, "and it won't be safe to stay that long. It might take a half hour to find all of 'em. We've got to get out of here quick and get some help."

Well, it certainly wasn't any time to argue, with maybe the whole $25,000 buried in the sawdust all around us. But we did have to decide whether to take what we'd found and beat it to camp and come back with help, or to dig up all the fish we could find right now, take the money out, shove it all into Little Jim's gunnysack, and come happily back into camp with every dollar of it.

Little Jim came up with a bright idea. "Let's dig up all the fish real quick, stuff 'em in my gunnysack, and beat it home to camp. We can take the money out on the way maybe—or else take the fish home for dinner."

I looked at his excited blue eyes and forgot that he was a goat. I thought how much I liked him.

"Boy!" he said, with a big grin on his mouse-like face. "Won't Mr. Ostberg be pleased to have his money back for the mission hospital!"

Here I'd been thinking about what a big reward Bill Collins was going to get for finding the money, and Little Jim wasn't thinking of himself at all. He was thinking of the folks in another land who needed the gospel for their souls and a doctor's help for their bodies. *What a great guy,* I thought.

But this story is long enough—and, anyway, that's really all there is to tell about how we found the ransom money. So I'll have to wind up the whole thing in another paragraph or two.

That wasn't the last exciting adventure we had on our northern camping trip, though, because a new and very dangerous adventure began to happen to us even before we got out of that old icehouse.

While we were digging and finding fish with sewed-up stomachs and stuffing them into Little Jim's gunnysack to take home to camp, suddenly I thought I heard a noise outside.

"*Sh!*" I said. "Somebody's coming!"

We all stood dead still and listened. And I

had heard a noise. Out on the lake there was the roar of a high-powered outboard motor that sounded as though it wasn't any more than a hundred yards from shore.

I could imagine that somebody on the other side of the lake had seen us and was coming across *roarety-sizzle* to stop whatever we were doing.

Little Jim grabbed up his stick. Poetry's grip tightened on his Scout knife handle till the knuckles on his hand turned white.

"Quick!" I said to all of us. "Let's get out of here with what we've got, or it'll be too late!"

I grabbed the gunnysack and lugged it toward the exit. All of us got there at about the same time. Boy oh boy, if only we could get out and make a dive for the woods and start to camp without being seen! That outboard motor was roaring toward our shore as though whoever was driving it was in a terrible hurry to stop us from doing whatever we were doing.

But as I said, this story is already finished, and what happened next is the beginning of another exciting adventure. Even while we were climbing out of that icehouse, I just knew that long before we got home with our ransom money, there'd be some dangerous excitement that would take not only a lot of quick thinking on the part of every one of us but some quick *acting* as well.

I hope I'll have time right away to tell you this last story of the Sugar Creek Gang's adventures in the north woods.

The *Sugar Creek Gang* Series: